Also by Andrew Nugent

Fiction
The Four Courts Murder
Second Burial for a Black Prince
Soul Murder

Spirituality
The Slow-Release Miracle

★

Praise for *The Four Courts Murder*

'It would take an iron will not to find oneself swept along by
the pace at which the story is told . . . compelling.'
—*The Irish Times*

'Excellent . . . Nugent deploys all the intellect and linguistic
brilliance required of his former profession, coupled with the
deep humour, understanding and genuine interest in his fellow
human beings essential to his vocation.'
—*The Guardian*

'Elegant, charming and clever . . . a novel as ingenious as it is
witty and compelling.'
—*The Irish Post*

First published in 2014 by
Liberties Press
140 Terenure Road North | Terenure | Dublin 6W
Tel: +353 (1) 405 5701
www.libertiespress.com | info@libertiespress.com

Trade enquiries to Gill & Macmillan Distribution
Hume Avenue | Park West | Dublin 12
T: +353 (1) 500 9534 | F: +353 (1) 500 9595 | E: sales@gillmacmillan.ie

Distributed in the United Kingdom by
Turnaround Publisher Services
Unit 3 | Olympia Trading Estate | Coburg Road | London N22 6TZ
T: +44 (0) 20 8829 3000 | E: orders@turnaround-uk.com

Distributed in the United States by
International Publishers Marketing
22841 Quicksilver Dr | Dulles, VA 20166
T: +1 (703) 661-1586 | F: +1 (703) 661-1547 | E: ipmmail@presswarehouse.com

ISBN: 978-1-909718-37-1
2 4 6 8 10 9 7 5 3 1

A CIP record for this title is available from the British Library.

Cover design by Liberties Press
Internal design, editing and typesetting by Liberties Press

This book, though a work of fiction, is based on the experiences of the author.

COMHAIRLE CHONTAE ÁTHA CLIATH THEAS
SOUTH DUBLIN COUNTY LIBRARIES

BALLYROAN BRANCH LIBRARY
TO RENEW ANY ITEM TEL: 494 1900
OR ONLINE AT www.southdublinlibraries.ie

Items should be returned on or before the last date below. Fines, as displayed in the Library, will be charged on overdue items.

For James and Margaret,
with all my love

PREFACE

The police procedural – so popular in our own day – is perhaps the modern and secular equivalent of the medieval morality play. In each of these genres, bad behaviour is recorded and punished, virtue is rewarded, and the scales of justice are thereby restored to equilibrium.

What matter if the Angel Gabriel is replaced in modern murder mysteries by Inspector Flatfoot? It is very much the mixture as before.

Of course, we don't quite believe either narrative, or, at least, what we do believe is that neither is the whole story. Sometimes, for instance, crime does pay, so routinely as to become almost – or even wholly – respectable. Just look around you!

From the vantage point of victims or survivors of crime, what happens or doesn't happen to villains, in the end, is merely the little story. Meanwhile, the victim or the survivor must often embark upon the hero's journey. This becomes their major preoccupation, even their life story.

Christopher Vogler has said, 'Heroes must die so that they can be reborn.' Perhaps the hero in each of us has to die so that another self can be born. A self that is worthy of the sacrifice.

That is the big story.

★

However, this book is not really a police procedural. Worse again, the 'hero', Eoin, is a celibate seminarian (without even the excuse of being gay – if you can believe him, that is). Nothing could be more counter-cultural at the present time. He is a *Narziss und Goldmund* character, bound inseparably with another chap, Andrew, who is an amateur womaniser (my own little joke).

Eoin and Andrew are my very self.

CHAPTER ONE

It was May 1968 – the year of the Student Revolution in France – and of a whole series of copycat hullabalaloos all over Europe. I had a walk-on part in this tragi-comedy/history-in-the-making, simply by being a student at Strasbourg University at that particular time.

Male, unattached, twenty-four years of age, I had been beavering away for most of a year at what might have become a doctoral thesis about a philosopher called Maurice Blondel. I did have interesting things to say about this chap. The only fly in the ointment was that at least half a dozen nerds had already said, and even written down, more or less the same great ideas as I had myself, and before I had got the chance to be the first, or even the second, to tell the world about them. That's academic life for you. It's like polar exploration. You've got to be the first! I had to content myself with a Master's degree in the end.

The word 'nerd' was not yet in common use in 1968. But intellectual integrity – that monkey on my back – obliges me to add a footnote to the effect that in those far-off days, I was actually a bit of a nerd myself. I must also confess that envy and jealousy are right up there with vanity and fornication when it comes to the besetting vices of academics. Do I need to personalise things any further? That is the kind of chap I was – then.

Academically, I was bright enough. At least, I had been told so fairly often by people who were supposed to know. Politically, on the other hand, I did not even know the facts of life. Of student issues specifically – and that is what May '68 was all about – I was abysmally ignorant and tone-deaf besides. A typical 'I'm-all-right-Jack', self-satisfied little git, I was not accustomed to bother about such things – if you are not itchy yourself, you do not feel like scratching.

I was, in fact, comfortably off, thanks to a legacy bequeathed for my studies by a rather dotty grand-aunt, who happened also to be dotty about me – which proves that she really was dotty. Meanwhile, I was genuinely interested in what I was doing, and I did not want to waste any of Grand Auntie's doubloons, or my own precious time. So I saw no necessity at all for any extraneous factor – like a mere revolution – to get in the way of my golden prospects. My only enthusiasms – apart from philosophy – were sports of all kinds, women and beer. I guess you could call me normal.

Was it mere coincidence that May 1968, and the twelve months that followed it, was probably the most formative stage in my entire life? It was during that time that I came to be – or was obliged to become more like the person that I hope I am now. Quite simply, I had to grow up, and stop being such a total – well, let's just say such a shallow individual.

Somebody was murdered. I add this almost casually, as if it were an afterthought. It is anything but that. It is, in fact, what this writing is all about. I am not ready to go there – not yet anyhow – but I will come to it soon, when I have set the stage properly, and, so to speak, taken several deep breaths.

I cannot pretend to be a historian, a sociologist, a political scientist, a head shrinker, or anything else clever like that, which could give me some special insight into how the planet creaks on its hinges. I can only tell you about how the events of that month impacted on me and on people whom I love, and how I became aware of events going on around me, and how I tried to understand them – and to act.

How did it all begin? I honestly don't know. Suddenly world history seemed to barge into my life, uninvited. First one trivial incident, then another, then a third. A few students got themselves arrested on some footling charge. What else is new? I think that the police invaded the university campus – at Nanterre, or was it the Sorbonne? Well, that *was* new. This had never been done before, even back to the dawn of history, the twelfth century, or whenever universities were invented. The universities have always been treated like holy places, like churches, or girls' dormitories, or the houses of parliament. They are total no-go areas for smelly police forces.

The first I heard of 'the Student Revolution' was when I looked up from the book I had been reading in the small library of the faculty of Protestant Theology at the university. It was exactly eleven o'clock. I even remember looking at my watch and humming some lines from a children's nursery rhyme, 'Here we go gathering nuts in May'. I must be psychic, because I realised just then that some nut was indeed beginning to address us that bright morning in May.

I actually knew the guy to see – even to nod to. He was from the *Grand Séminaire* near the cathedral. Like all seminarians in

11

Alsace, Catholic and Protestant, he was obliged by concordat between the French State and Church authorities to do his theological studies at the university. Presumably, this was so that he could both learn to serve God diligently and, at the same time, be taught not to rock the ship of state more than was respectable and wise.

This chap was a heavy-set, stocky type, quite square in shape – due, no doubt, to a youth spent shovelling *choucroute* and Black Forest gateau into his mouth, and washing it down with generous infusions of Kronenbourg or Mutzig.

I actually owed a new French word to this particular Alsatian. I was so fascinated by an aspect of his appearance that I looked it up specially in the dictionary. The word was '*aisselles*', which means 'armpits'. Not that either of this boy's armpits was particularly alluring or remarkable in any way, except that, summer or winter, they each presided over a triangular swamp of odoriferous sweat measuring, it seemed to me, a good quarter acre. You could not help looking at him – which, from the point of view of speech-making, was probably an advantage. His *aisselles* alone assured him of a captive, if slightly horrified, audience. Besides, once he had got you hooked, he did not let you go. He was, I have to confess, a compelling speaker.

He was asking us on this May morning, with controlled passion – which was even more effective than unbridled heat – to 'strike a blow' for our 'imprisoned brothers'. No doubt, there had been a whole pre-history to this thing. But that was the first I had heard of what was about to be a real-life revolution – one to which I was just about to be invited.

Perhaps the guy was a hypnotist, who, having riveted our attention, not by dangling a pendulum under our noses, but by dint of his soggy underarms, was now continuing to cast a spell on his captive audience, making us all feel 'fraternal'.

He conjured up lurid images of the Bastille (which, according to my information, had in fact been razed to the ground two hundred years ago, in the amateurish dress rehearsal for *our* great about-to-be revolution). No matter! We could see vividly, down into the dark and dank bowels of *some* Bastille somewhere, and somehow come to life again, brutality, starvation, thumbscrews, things horrible and obscene beyond belief – once they had got the baby-soft flesh of our 'imprisoned brothers' down into their ghastly dungeons. We had to do *something*!

The blow to be struck for these imprisoned brothers of ours, according to this orator, was, very appropriately, to go on strike ourselves. We, and thousands of other students who, we were assured, had been listening simultaneously to other spokespersons for *Liberté, Égalité et Fraternité* – would be doing precisely the same thing from the following morning. It was humbling to know that this major logistical exercise had all been arranged – by dark of night, no doubt – by *le syndicat des étudiants*, the students union, a body of which I had never even heard until just now.

It came as a relief – almost an anti-climax – to hear that all we were being asked to do at this juncture was not to go to lectures on the following morning, but to stay in our beds instead, and perhaps on other days as well. This was well within the range of the idealism and the generosity of the average student. Personally, I was quite happy to do, and to die, and to give all (strictly within the limits of the suggested parameters) to *'faire grasse matinée'*, meaning, to have a jolly good lie-in the next morning.

And so we did go on strike, though very unevenly nationwide, it must be admitted. The imprisoned students were promptly released, on some face-saving pretext from the point of view of the authorities. Those heroes – there were no heroines for the moment – had not had their fingernails pulled out, been beaten with chains, starved, castrated, or maltreated in any way. Nevertheless, to my astonishment, the strike continued, grew wings, gathered momentum, and within days, dominated national politics.

The French expression for going on strike is '*faire la grève*', which means, roughly, 'doing the gravel beach thing'. Coincidentally, or by some mysterious alchemy of history, this curious phrase has its origins in another student strike that occurred more than seven hundred years before *our* one, which surely proves that history does repeat itself, at least sometimes.

On Shrove Tuesday, 1229, some students of the University of Paris, who had been drinking much more than was good for their little tummies, turned bolshie and refused to pay the innkeeper his lawful entitlement. When the innkeeper responded by getting stroppy in turn, the students beat him up, together with most of the other customers in his tavern. A riot ensued.

After a whole succession of tit-for-tat incidents between town and gown during the following weeks – and even months – the authorities decided that enough was enough, and that they would teach the students a lesson. This was, no doubt, as is usual on such occasions, '*pour encourager les autres*'. They went too far. The result was that half a dozen students lay dead. They were not even the same ones who had caused all the trouble in the first place.

The students were outraged. To show their indignation at what the authorities had done to their pals, they went down to the gravelly beaches that bordered the River Seine in those days, and sat gloomily there for the next two years. This was ample time for the expression *'faire la grève'* to enter irrevocably into the bloodstream of the French language. In the meantime, business was very bad for all kinds of people.

At the end of two years, some of the students sensibly decided to get on with the rest of their lives. So, exclaiming *'Merde Alors!'* – which has also passed into the student vernacular – they decamped to Toulouse, where they founded a brand new university, with some help from the Pope, who presumably took an indulgent view of their coarse language and general lifestyle.

Whether lying on the beaches or lying in their beds, students can make of their strikes tenacious affairs. Personally, having 'done and died' and lain in bed once, I was all set to fast-forward the rest of the revolution. I was also beginning to be exasperated. Though comparatively well-off by student standards, I could certainly not afford the luxury of being held up in my studies for two years, with the further prospect of having eventually to found my own university, with or without help from the reigning Pontiff.

France may be *'le pays de Descartes'*, but that does not mean that the French are always very logical. We had been asked to go on strike to secure the release of our student buddies. We did go on strike. The students were freed. And then what did we do? We stayed on strike and even tried to get as many *real* workers as possible to join our gang. 'What on earth was that all about?' I wondered truculently. It was from that point onwards that I thought that the students had lost the plot and were just being bloody-minded.

I think now – forty years later – that I was wrong. The fact is – as I have said – that I was quite comfortably off, supported by reasonably well-to-do parents and a dotty and doting grand aunt. And I was also a beneficiary of a partial scholarship from La Ville de Strasbourg. I was somebody who did not feel student issues '*tripalement*' – another fine word, invented during our revolution. It means 'in the tripes' or, as we would say nowadays, 'in the gut'. I did not feel these things in my tripes or in my guts because, as a privileged spectator, I did not need to feel anything at all, either in my bowels or even in my brain. That is not a good way to be.

My guess now about the seemingly illogical prolongation of the strike is that the students had been amazed by the release of 'our imprisoned brothers'. The discovery that someone, somewhere, had actually listened to the students, indeed had been *forced* to listen to them, even briefly, about something, anything – that just went to the students' heads. If they could secure the release of their companions by going on strike, then what about all of those other issues where they had been systematically ignored and not listened to since – it seemed – the dawn of human history?

I knew just enough about the students' problems to recognise that they were chronic, endemic, and insoluble, to the point that I – with self-centred alacrity – and the students themselves – with patient resignation – assumed that this was how student life had always been, and would forever continue to be until the end of time.

There was tremendous overcrowding, inadequate domestic and academic accommodation, insufficient recreational facilities and too many lazy, venal, or simply brain-dead teachers. Most galling of all, perhaps, was the mindless centralisation, that made it impossible for officials on the ground to introduce even the simplest remedies for local problems and frustrations.

All these causes of dissatisfaction had been made worse by

the mushrooming of student numbers since the early nineteen-sixties. This was because of the abrupt end of the dirty war in Algeria and the proclamation of independence for that former French colony. These events had been followed by a massive influx to mainland France of '*pieds-noirs*' – colonial French, who did not wish to live under an Arab regime. Incidentally, they were called '*pieds-noirs*' by the Arabs, not because their feet were particularly dirty, but simply because of their fondness for wearing black leather shoes.

These ex-colonials, together with French-born ex-soldiers whose studies had been delayed or interrupted by the war, constituted an indigestible lump throughout the French educational system, and especially at third level.

Besides, most of these *pieds-noirs* and ex-soldiers loathed Charles de Gaulle, the President of the French Republic. Having proclaimed from the housetops '*Algérie Française*' and persuaded them to put their lives on the line for the defence of a French Algeria, he had stabbed them in the backs – as they saw it anyhow – and done a deal with the devil. I personally knew a couple of chaps who had been young officers in the French army in Algeria. These *garçons* – and they were little more than boys – had been stranded out in the desert for weeks on end, surrounded by Arab 'French' soldiers, who knew perfectly well that de Gaulle was playing a double game. Night after night, these young officers would lay down to sleep in their tents, never knowing when their soldiers would come to slit their throats and sneak away to the other side.

These young fellows realised, too, that their soldiers would *have* to do this sooner or later, to escape the inevitable reprisals awaiting Arabs who had dawdled too long with the colonial power. Algeria was a dirty war, with no mercy shown on either side. General Massu, the French Commander, had made no bones about authorising torture as a legitimate, indeed, the only, means to secure victory. What a dilemma for young Frenchmen to be caught up in, serving such a ruthless regime! Many of them never forgave de Gaulle for it.

Suddenly, in May '68, for these or other reasons, or for no reasons at all, the students flipped their collective lid. It was spring, of course, and – as I knew only too well from personal experience – in that particular season, students are prone to sudden rushes of blood to various parts of the anatomy. Come spring, strange things do happen in the undergraduate world – and even in the graduate world. Students throw buckets of water at each other, out of windows, or off flat roofs. They streak. They moon – not just as in moping about the place, but as in exposing their nether regions to the elements, and to other people, who invariably act horrified. They talk unreasonably loudly, sing '*des paillards*' (bawdy songs) in raucous choruses, and giggle hysterically for no apparent reason. And, of course, they dream impossible dreams.

Sexual and social frustration certainly played a part, especially at Nanterre. This was a vast university campus, accommodating more than twelve thousand students, housed in dirty concrete-block buildings, slapped down in the midst of '*taudisvilles*' (shanty towns) and rubbish dumps on the western fringe of Paris. Incredibly, male students were refused all access to female residences – on the assumption that all they could possibly have on their minds, if they ever *did* get in there, would be non-stop fornication. This, accordingly, became a self-fulfilling prophecy. Young people are so inclined to live either up or down to their elders' expectations.

If Nanterre was to become the powder-keg of the revolution,

this – initially, anyhow – was not caused by a simple burst of bad behaviour because of local conditions. The students were not rebelling against an insufficiency of urinals – or even condoms. It was the shape of the wider world that was bugging them. They were identifying with so many of the themes of an international youth movement, which felt and knew that their elders – the movers and shakers of international power politics – could, and should, be doing better. These young people were anti-capitalist, anti-imperialist, anti-paternalist, and, above all – a focus for so much else that was patently wrong with the world of that time – anti the war in Vietnam.

The government, for its part, totally underestimated these particular students, at that particular season, and in that particular year. Nobody seemed to understand the power of their idealism, the depths of their pent-up frustrations and the strength of their stormy emotions. Knowing so little about the ins and outs of student politics, even I could see that Alain Peyrefitte, the Minister for Education – a very bright man, who was expected to go far – would not, in fact, go any further, at least not in national politics. He did write at least two very good books after that and, no doubt, did many other interesting things in his life, but he was to be one of the first political casualties of the Revolution. The peremptory way in which he said the single word '*Écoutez*' (Listen!) to the students – I can still hear him saying it on the radio – showed clearly that he himself was incapable of hearing anything that they had wanted to say to him.

I suppose, too, that the students wanted more money. Most people usually do. Strange though, I don't remember hearing much about money at the time. All the stress was on '*participation*', '*dialogue*', and '*solidarité*'. Of course, we are talking French here, and such words take on an almost sensuous, even volup-

tuous nuance in that language. These concepts, or, better, aspi-
rations, are utterly opposed to '*paternalisme*', with all its
Freudian, ball-crushing, heavy-handed associations. The
French educational system – at all levels – was extraordinarily
hidebound and absurdly paternalistic. It was said that if a primary school in the foothills of the Pyrenees wanted an extra
sheet of lavatory paper, they would have to apply, in triplicate,
to Paris, where the appropriate official would wrestle with the
Lord in prayer about all aspects of the problem. Would conced-
ing a spare scrap of tissue create a precedent? Would it – to use
an unfortunate metaphor – open the floodgates?

In a word – in a lot of words, actually, because this had to be
the wordiest revolution in history – the students wanted the
most radical change of all: they wanted to be consulted. They
wanted to be *listened to*.

That was a new one on Charles de Gaulle. Like Mr de Valera
on our own landing strip – I am Irish, by the way – he thought
that it was quite enough by way of consultation if he looked
into his own heart. Le Grand Charles was routinely depicted in
the pages of *Le Canard Enchainé*, the hugely influential satirical
newspaper, as *Le Roi Soleil*, Louis XIV. Imperious, nose in the air
– and that was some schnozzle – adorned in full-bottomed wig,
equipped with grandee's staff and *lorgnette*, all the better to
inspect the lower forms of life, meaning you and me. Arrogant,
vain, and conceited.

On the other hand, de Gaulle was no fool, either. In the first
days of the revolution he simply disappeared, while the students, drunk on hubris and plonk, ran amok – cavorting in the
streets, making love in their lecture halls, creating dung-heaps
and public lavatories wherever they went. And, meanwhile, de
Gaulle bided his time.

Not all the students behaved badly. For instance, there were the seminarians. The University of Strasbourg is a Reformation foundation with a German-style concordatory relationship with the churches, whereby all Christian clergy of the diocese are obliged to attend the state faculties of Protestant or Catholic theology. In Alsace at that time there were numerous vocations. Moreover, there were plenty of young seminarians from other dioceses in France, and also from abroad, attracted by the ready-made concentration of like-minded people, as also by the facilities of theological faculties backed by the finances of the French Republic.

The relevance of these factors to the events of May 1968 is that there were a large number of seminarians, both Catholic and Protestant, who had already been whipped up to a white heat of excitement by the recent Second Vatican Council. These youths sincerely believed that if only they could kick up everything into the air, once and for all, it would necessarily come down again in the shape of heaven on earth. In equal parts innocent, charming and utterly guileless, they took to the student revolution with all the missionary zeal of ducks to water – and just as inconsequentially.

Alas, the end of this unsatisfactory world did not ineluctably follow, as they had hoped. Disillusioned, not a few of those ingenuous young men went into a sulk, and thence to a depression. They abandoned their seminaries, their celibacy and even their churches. I was not much older myself than most of those seminarians but – even then – I knew that they were hopelessly and helplessly naive. And yet, in my heart, I envied them. I should have been with them, hoping against hope.

Strasbourg was one of the places where the revolutionaries were most ardent and most active. By 1968, most of the faculties had got new buildings on the Esplanade, east of the city. But the *Palais Universitaire* in the centre of town, with its imposing entrance and statues of Reformation figures on top of the facade, was still the symbolic headquarters of the university. It was occupied at dawn on Saturday 11 May by latter-day Jacobins who raised the red flag on the roof.

The previous night had been *La Nuit des Barricades* in Paris, when, finally, strutting and posturing had spilled over into naked violence. Students ripped up the paving stones in the Latin quarter, hurling half of them at the police, and building at least sixty barricades with the rest. These barricades were reinforced with litter bins, fences torn down, anything and everything to be grabbed in haste from building sites, and with upturned cars – nearly two hundred of them were damaged or destroyed in that one night.

The police responded with tear gas, and with violent baton charges. The battle raged through the night. Eventually, the students were driven from their cover. Then the real savagery began. Residents of the Latin Quarter, appalled by the police behaviour, tried in vain to shield the students from the fury of rifle-butts and truncheons. Even Red Cross stretcher-bearers were attacked, their wounded youngsters dragged away for further beating. At the end of that night there were 367 wounded, and 460 taken into custody. It is said that, of the 367 wounded, 251 were policemen or employees of other public services. Those figures are highly suspect. A member of the CRS, who could perfectly legitimately lay claim to some paid sick leave, was much more likely to allow himself to be carried away on a stretcher than a student who knew that if he did the same, he would probably be dragged off his stretcher and beaten again, investigated, then possibly charged or even deported. No student who was at least able to hobble wanted his name to feature in police records.

The Strasbourg students had been following events in Paris all night on their radios with mounting anger. Already by 5.30 in the morning, when *Danny-le Rouge* (Daniel Cohn-Bendit), the student leader at Paris – and now a respected member of the European Parliament – had given the order to disperse, the students at Strasbourg had seized the *Palais Universitaire*. The revolution had arrived on our doorstep.

Three days after the students had seized possession of the *palais*, the CRS arrived by dark of night and threw a ring of steel around the building. The forces of law and order in France, as in many countries, are reluctant to invade temples, churches, and seats of learning. As has been said, this immunity from profanation goes back a long way. Besides, the authorities were not anxious to arrest students – as they knew perfectly well that the courts would have let them out again with minimum ceremony. And anyhow, the ring of steel acted as a very effective form of de facto imprisonment, because no student who was already inside the *Palais Universitaire* would have dared to come out again, unless he could run very fast indeed. The one or two who tried, but didn't make it, were not arrested or charged with any offence: they merely had the crap beaten out of them.

Meanwhile, in buildings with free access, as in buildings occupied by the students and surrounded by riot police, the interminable chin-wagging went on day and night. The Hegelian dialectic of '*thèse*' and '*antithèse*' was most often completed, not by '*synthèse*' – as it should be – but by '*foutaise*'. This means, in vulgar language, absolute bullshit.

I attended a few of these rave-ins and found them amusing, or even intriguing in the short term. But, almost always, after twenty minutes, it seemed like I had strayed into the Annual General Meeting of the Headbangers Association. What was passing before my eyes, and in one ear and out the other, was a swollen stream of unconsciousness. The whole exercise – known by the impressive title of *'dialogue permanent'* – was, in fact, a monumental self-inflicted filibuster. The only aspect that I could identify as 'permanent' was the persistent assumption that meaning could be conveyed to an audience without the mediation of coherent words or ideas; and anyhow, most of the audience was simply not listening.

I gave a speech myself one night about the importance of believing in Santa Claus. It was punctuated by cries of 'Heil Hitler' from three or four lusty lads, who would leap to their feet and perform the appropriate liturgical honours. Another student – a girl this time – peppered my oration with shrill reprises of *Oh la vache, la vache*! Try as I could, I was not able to see the relevance of either intervention. I spoke first in French, then slipped successively into English, Irish, Latin, and bad German. It did not make the slightest difference, except that the 'Heil Hitler' brigade redoubled their efforts on hearing the bad German, and the 'La Vache' lady went up several decibels at the sound of the Gaelic.

A subsequent speaker berated me for talking Mandarin when, he said, I knew perfectly well that the solid citizens of Alsace only spoke the Chinese of the Delta. 'What "Delta"?' I tried to ask, on a point of information, but was howled down. That does give some idea of what *dialogue permanent* was like. I have always been allergic to meetings – pretty well *all* meetings – ever since.

A few earnest, eager, or frankly weird lecturers strayed into one or other of these Mad Hatter's tea parties. They were mostly treated insultingly – like the accused at the show trials fashionable in China at that time. For all their pains, these academics did not manage to advance whatever cause they were championing one whit, let alone the sum total of human wisdom. Two of the more prominent figures who made hopeful entrances and precipitate exits, to and from the Sorbonne at Paris, were François Mitterrand, subsequently President of the French Republic, and Jean-Paul Sartre, who must have been particularly peeved by the almost derisory reception he received. Only one month previously, Sartre could well have regarded himself as the quasi-official *enfant terrible* of the Latin Quarter.

The students were no respecters of persons. The rare politicians or 'great thinkers' who seemed to assume that they could score in some way, or get notional inside track with the students, almost all exited again rapidly, badly mauled moralewise, though not, of course, physically. To the students' credit, it must be said that there was little intentional violence against persons during May 1968. The same cannot be said for elements within the forces of law and order, some of whom were clearly determined to teach this '*marmaille*' (gaggle of brats) a lesson they would never forget.

During the second Night of the Barricades (23 May), the CRS, who admittedly had been under enormous strain for nearly three weeks, finally went berserk. That day, and for several days following, they terrorised both activist and innocent students indiscriminately – even young teens on their way to school, who had nothing whatsoever to do with the revolution. They seized the youngsters' bicycles, ripped up the tyres, emptied their school books into the street, beat them, and even lined them up on the side of the street to ritually kick them all in the testicles.

The police arrested people on a completely arbitrary basis. Anyone with a foreign name or a funny accent or who, for whatever reason, did not please the CRS, would be rounded up and routinely brutalised, punched, kicked, and made to run a gauntlet where faces were smashed and ribs broken. At Beaujon Hospital, which served as a detention centre, they threatened their captives with further beatings, and prevented them from calling their families or receiving medical attention.

Meanwhile, Charles de Gaulle bided his time very patiently – until he was quite sure that 'les braves français' had had more than enough of bad behaviour from the students, and that all the other politicians had made complete asses of themselves. Then he suddenly reappeared and gathered his children around him for a little fireside chat, via radio and television.

De Gaulle had not been twiddling his thumbs in idleness during the period of his invisibility. He had secretly flown to Baden-Baden to assure himself with the French Forces in Germany, and with General Jacques Massu, the 'Sledgehammer of Algeria', that, if push came to shove, they would stand behind him. After all, this was the era of '*The Day of the Jackal*' when, precisely because of Algeria, assassination attempts on de Gaulle were frequent. They almost always had a dissident military – and therefore a highly expert – hardcore behind them.

Eventually, in return for an amnesty promised to General Raoul Salan and other rebels and conspirators – still sore about Algeria – de Gaulle had received an absolute and unconditional promise of loyalty from the army. With this in his pocket, he returned to Paris.

There was another possible reason for the flight into

Germany: de Gaulle left France precisely so that he could come back there again. He was symbolically re-enacting what he had done in 1944, on 25 August – the feast of St Louis, King of France. Then he had entered Paris to liberate the city and the nation from the tyranny of Nazism. He was entering Paris once again from abroad in May '68, to liberate France, this time from the tyranny of anarchy. It would be the performance of his life.

De Gaulle was both *'superbe'* and *'sublime'*, in the best seventeenth-century sense of those very French words, that imply an almost toxic mixture of pride, courage and noble ambition. God knows the man had style: he would tell the nation the facts of life and give it to them straight from the shoulder. De Gaulle was convinced that the French people had had a bellyful of what most solid citizens viewed with distaste as adolescent cat-farting. Satisfied, too, that the trade unions, and particularly the Communist party, hated like hell having to play second fiddle to what they regarded as a soft-balled spew of mummies' darlings, he was also shrewdly aware that the students themselves had no intention that their heroism get in the way of their summer jobs or vacations. He sent the whole nation off to the seaside with this *superbe* and *sublime* challenge ringing in their ears: *'La Réforme, Oui: Le Chienlit, Non!'*

Fifty million *françaises* and *français* scrambled for their dictionaries, to see what *'chienlit'* meant. Nobody knew. Etymologically, the word, in fact, means the unseemly behaviour of one who shits in his own bed. This was felt to sum up the situation admirably. It was the beginning of the end for the student revolution.

When the trade unions eventually refused to back *'les fils à papa'*, or mummies' darlings, Georges Pompidou, the Prime Minister, who had meanwhile returned from a leisurely trip around Iran and Afghanistan, engaged the students in face-to-face, friendly conversations. He gave them hope, that their grievances would be listened to and remedied.

When de Gaulle called a snap election in June, the result was a massive parliamentary majority for the Gaullists. The student revolution was as dead as the dodo.

The sequel is truly amazing. De Gaulle overplayed his hand as recklessly as a student revolutionary himself. Afflicted, it must be, with full-blown 'folie de grandeur', and sincerely believing that someone as large as himself could actually walk on water, he fired Pompidou – the one man in his administration who genuinely had both the common touch and an effective avuncular rapport with the students – who liked and trusted him. Worse, de Gaulle replaced Pompidou as Prime Minister with the dowdy Maurice Couve de Murville, who probably did not want the job anyway, and lasted less than a year in it.

When, one year later, Pompidou was being installed as President of France, de Gaulle was to be seen morosely plodding along the misty moors of Kerry and Mayo. Ireland – rather incredibly – was the land of some of his ancestors too, as well as of all those American presidents: Jack Kennedy, Richard Nixon, Ronald Reagan, and even Barack Obama. De Gaulle most probably did not really want to be in Ireland at that time, or indeed at any time, but he wanted even less to be in France for the installation of Georges Pompidou as President of France, whom the same '*Canard Enchainé*' had invariably caricatured as a little mannequin standing on de Gaulle's desk in the Élysée Palace, smoking one of those frightful Gauloises. That was probably how *Mon Général* preferred to remember his faithful poodle.

CHAPTER TWO

One way to learn history – the non-academic way – is to actually live through a slice of it. Of course, you don't usually realise that it is history at the time. If you had told me in May 1968 that I was living through history, I would have laughed out loud. May 1968 came to be fixed in my mind and memory forever, not so much as history, but because of things that happened in my own life at that time. If it is history, it is personal history, it is my history, and the history of people whom I loved and still love.

My own history is, admittedly, for anyone other than myself, less exciting than the Student Revolution. So, I'll give you the short version of it. I am Andrew Olden. My father, unhappily deceased, was always about to get down to the business of working out our family tree, but he never actually got around to it. He said that we came from Normandy in the twelfth century. But, between Normandy in the twelfth century, and yesterday – it seems – nothing special happened.

My mother, a fat and jolly woman (who would kill me for

that penpicture), professes complete ignorance and indifference about my father's pedigree. She seems to think that it suffices to say that he was 'a total sweetheart', which is certainly true, but does not get us much further in the matter of genealogy. I have an uncomfortable feeling that there may be a few skeletons in the family cupboard. Perhaps I am descended from a long line of hangmen or tax collectors, with one or more deft changes of religion or maybe politics along the way, motivated, of course, by crass expediency.

With that less than illustrious but honest introduction to who I *may* be, let me formally present Strasbourg on the Rhine, as the theatre for our segment of the Student Revolution. Strasbourg is the capital city of Alsace, a territory that has been ping-ponged back and forth repeatedly since the fourth century, between Lotharingia, Germany, and France. It is probably destined to be swapped yet again each time that the riparian protagonists have a lovers' quarrel. No wonder that Alsatians sound foreign whichever language they are speaking, French or German. Of course, they have their own language as well – Alsatian, a dialect of German – which I would have to describe as . . . very much an acquired taste. Not surprisingly, they do pretty well their own thing.

Strasbourg is a city of about a quarter of a million people. Founded by the Romans in 15 BC, it is worldly-wise, having seen more or less everything in its long history. It has atmosphere and poise. It is beautiful – whether it be the soaring gothic cathedral in red sandstone, the *Château des Rohan* or the old houses of *La Petite France* with their gourmet restaurants, which, unfortunately, I could not afford more than rarely. According to the touristy postcards, every chimney-stack on the more traditional houses has a large circular nest obstructing it, with a stork embedded in it – as we say about journalists – and just about to lay an enormous egg. The storks, silly, not the journalists. I found myself initially worrying about how the smoke gets out of the fireplaces, or Santa Claus gets in.

Since 1949, Strasbourg has been the seat of the Council of Europe, and since 1979, the site of the European Parliament.

During *les évènements* of 1968, the notes for my thesis were trapped inside the Palais Universitaire, where they were quite inaccessible, because of the presence of the CRS, who would have cheerfully disembowelled any student attempting to get in or out of the building. Fortunately, I was assured by the librarian that the notes were safely under lock and key in the library of the faculty of Catholic theology. She had been one of the last people out of the Palais Universitaire, before the arrival of the CRS, and she had extracted a promise from the students to respect the library. Indeed, it was the students themselves who had encouraged her to make the library secure. At least I had the satisfaction of knowing that my precious notes were safely beyond the reach of anyone who might be tempted to use them for inappropriate purposes. The students did suffer severe and distressing shortages – of lavatory paper, for instance – during what was, in effect, an all-out siege.

In the meantime, I could have gone ahead with other areas of my project at the *Bibliothèque Nationale* on the *Place de la République*, scarcely half a mile away from the faculty. It was Eoin Macklin who persuaded me to take a break from it all.

I seem to have known Eoin since almost before I was born. The same age as myself – I was the elder by two months – he lived in the next street to me, growing up in the pleasant Dublin suburb of Mount Merrion. Our parents were friends. We attended the same primary and secondary schools, played on the same rugby and soccer teams, and hung out with the same gang of boys and girls. After leaving school, Eoin had done one year of a General Arts degree at University College Dublin. Then, he amazed us all by deciding to enter a religious order. As a pal said to me at the time, 'There he was, sitting up on a high stool in O'Dwyer's, only last week, drinking his pint – perfectly normal, nothing in the wide world wrong with him – and then, *this*! Jaysus, it would make you think!'

Eoin had always been part of the furniture of my life. I took him completely for granted. We discussed everything together and had no secrets from one another – well, until this thing. I suppose it was a decision that he had to work out for himself, and perhaps I should not have been so surprised. I missed him terribly.

Inevitably, I lost track of my friend for a few years. I suppose he was doing his basic training in spiritual warfare, or whatever they do. Then, lo and behold, his religious congregation sent him to Strasbourg, to study theology at the same university in exactly the same month and year as myself, October 1967. I was so happy to meet up with him again, and delighted to find that, in spite of being hijacked by the God squad, he was exactly the same good guy that I had always known. Our enthusiasms were, no doubt, a little different by then. I won't dwell on my own, which I suppose were fairly predictable – namely beer and girls, in that order, of course. It is said that in Ireland, a 'queer' is a guy who prefers girls to beer.

Eoin, I remember, was all worked up about the Vatican Council, which was just finishing around that time. He seemed to think – like all those other dudes in his seminary – that the

Council was the immediate hors d'oeuvre for the heavenly banquet. I was not so sure about that. As a sort of outside observer, I would have thought that the Church's problems were only beginning, once they had, at long last, made up their minds to join the real world, and that is what I think the Vatican Council was meant to be all about. I did not say this to Eoin, of course. Why hurt his feelings? I was quite sure about two things: firstly, he was one hell of a nice guy, and secondly – whether he was right or whether he was wrong about these things – he was always utterly sincere.

Eoin was living in the *Séminaire International* in rue Beethoven, only ten minutes walk from the faculty, and beside a pleasant park called the *Orangerie*. Napoléon had built a pavilion in this park for the Empress Marie-Louise, on his way eastwards on his ill-fated excursion to Moscow. The *Séminaire* provided a residence for some dozens of clerical students from up to fifteen nations and also for French seminarians from outside the Strasbourg diocese.

During the second world war, the building had served as a club for German officers – 'club' probably being a bit of a euphemism. It was more likely a glorified brothel. In Eoin's time, some of the plates and saucers were still emblazoned with the swastika. I badly wanted to pocket one of these as a souvenir. Eoin was shocked, so I restrained myself, and suffered the frustration of knowing, for sure, that they would all have disappeared within a year or two. And, of course, I was right. The seminary itself has long since vanished too, having been levelled to make way for of luxury apartments.

God rewarded Eoin for his honesty – at my expense – in the matter of the flying – or disappearing – saucers. One day, while hiking in the Vosges foothills, he found an alternative keepsake of the Third Reich. Having retired behind a blackberry bush for a call of nature, he spotted something glinting in the middle of the tangled brambles. He hauled this object out, and found himself the proud possessor of a German helmet, exactly as depicted in all those second world war movies. The helmet was in quite good condition, even two decades after the war – as befitted something made by the master-race – except that it had two neat bullet holes where the frontal lobe of the brain would have been. This meant, paradoxically, that somebody had found the last wearer's Achilles heel. It had most probably been shot off his head, and had lain there for almost a quarter of a century – since the Battle of the Bulge, the last major German counter-offensive of the war on the Western front.

This helmet was, for Eoin, a treasured trophy. I don't know what happened to it eventually, but I would have very much liked to have had it – not so much as a souvenir of warfare, but as something strangely redeemed from its sinister uses by having made Eoin happy.

Initially, neither he nor I had known that the other was in Strasbourg. We literally bumped into one another on the stairway in rue Beethoven. What a huge and happy surprise! An extraordinary man, Le Père Vincent Ou was both spiritual director at the *Séminaire*, and a chaplain at the University Parish. It was when I was trying to do something tentative about my own spiritual life – such as it was – that Père Ou's dual role brought Eoin and myself together again.

I have described Père Ou as an extraordinary man, and he was. About five feet high and a sartorial disaster, he was also of the highest Chinese aristocracy – a son or grandson of the Grand Vizier to the last Emperor of China. He had come to France as a young man to study mathematics, and had there been converted to Catholicism and been ordained a priest. In the meantime, Mao Tse-tung had done his Long March, and China had become a Communist empire. Père Ou was never to see his country or his family again. He was a wonderful influence on those of us so fortunate as to fall under his spell. Profoundly spiritual, intellectually brilliant, comical, his own man, and as innocent as a new-born baby.

The seminary was a friendly place. Often in the evening I would drop in for a chat with Eoin. The events of May 1968 found the seminarians no less polarised than the rest of the student body. Some of these guys had served in the French army at the tail-end of the Algerian war. Even those who had not been soldiers were mostly for change, and against the status quo. Many of them were very active in the student revolution.

On one occasion, Eoin had met de Gaulle face to face. A group of seminarians was at Strasbourg train station to travel to Selestat for a cultural outing. Their train was delayed, because President de Gaulle was arriving from Paris, and no train could be permitted to pass his – in either direction – on the adjoining track. This, I repeat, was *Day of the Jackal* fever time, when attempts on the President's life were a real possibility. Once safely arrived in Alsace, de Gaulle would be assured of a warm welcome. The solid citizens of Strasbourg adored him, because, for a start, they were right-wing anyhow, and then, because he had succeeded in preventing the Americans from bombing their city at the end of the war to dislodge the Germans, who had reoccupied Strasbourg.

But, on that day, all of the French seminarians had gone into a bistro to drink beer, rather than have it said that they had come to greet their favourite hate-figure. Eoin, who did not have anything against de Gaulle – or indeed against anyone else in the whole wide world – remained in the crowd and was there when de Gaulle arrived soon afterwards.

True to form – and to the manifest dismay of his anxious minders – *Mon Général* instantly plunged into the mob of faithful followers and curious tourists, eager to catch a glimpse of yet another ancient monument. He shook hands ardently to the right and left of him, and seemed oblivious to all dangers. That, too, it appears, was one of his little vanities. He took risks, and was at times quite reckless. Perhaps this is because he knew, perfectly well, that even God could not do without him.

Eoin was very blonde, and clearly not French. The President shook hands with him and asked where he was from. Eoin said that he was from Ireland. De Gaulle held him at arm's length and studied his face. Then he said pleasantly: '*Tiens! Moi aussi!*' and, seeing Eoin's amazement, he added, '*Veuillez le croire, mon brave, veuillez le croire!*', which could be rendered in modern Mid-Atlantic as 'Me too, dude! You'd better believe it!'

It was typical of Eoin that he did not repeat this conversation to his companions when they emerged from their bistro, correctly intuiting that any one of at least three dozen aspects of that short exchange might vex them exceedingly. Young French males had a very Oedipal relationship with the father-figure of the French Republic at that time.

Eoin did make three pragmatic observations about his encounter.

(1) 'I knew that he was very tall. I never realised that he is enormously fat as well.'

(2) 'His eyes are incredibly old, and as lacklustre as hard-boiled sweets.'

(3) 'His hands were like shovels; like the hands on Michelangelo's *David*.'

That was Eoin; he really saw things – and people. Who else in the world would have seen any resemblance between Michelangelo's *David* and General de Gaulle?

Meanwhile the French seminarians were being highly indignant about having missed such an excellent sighting of the devil incarnate – and even his handshakes. They immediately added this 'slight', as they saw it, to the list of grievances that made of de Gaulle *'un grand salaud'*! In the Irish vernacular of the time, this was 'a dirty louser'. That he had not even shaken hands with them! Once again, whoever said that France is *'le pays de Descartes'*, meaning that the French have a tendency to be logical, needs his head examined.

Two weeks into the revolution, it had already become clear that there would be no more teaching at the university in that academic year. Moreover, there would not be examinations either. This would be a major inconvenience, particularly for foreign students facing their finals. They would have to prolong their stay in France until the autumn, or return there at considerable expense to do their finals. Eoin had a proposal.

'Andrew, how would you be fixed for a complete tour of France, I mean, hitch-hiking?'

'What for?' I asked.

'To see the sights and to learn the language.'

'We already know the language,' I protested.

'No, we don't, Andy. We understand our lectures and what we read. That is far from possessing a language from the inside, the way we can speak it without thinking up what we are going to say in advance.'

'Is that really desirable?' I asked sarcastically.

'Yes, it is. That is when we really discover what we are thinking. It comes as a surprise to us. So much of our deep reflection goes on in our subconscious. It slips out when we are least expecting it. I know a guy who says that there are three tests about whether you *really* know a language.'

'Yeah, what are they?' I inquired, still sceptical.

'One, is if you can understand cinema and television. Two, is if you can eavesdrop on a conversation between several people at the next table, or behind you.'

'Both difficult,' I agreed, more reasonably, because people do talk in shorthand most of the time. 'So what is the third test?'

'The third test is: do you dream in that language?'

'Dream?!' I exclaimed, surprised and interested.

'Yes, that shows that the language has really sunk into your subconscious.'

Something must have sunk into my subconscious. That night I dreamt that Eoin was dead. It was horrible. I could not shake that sick feeling off for days. At one point, I even found myself crying. I never told Eoin about that dream. My instinct was that we would both have found it acutely embarrassing, that neither of us would have known where to look. I guess that Eoin knows about it now, and he understands.

We continued our conversation about how well we both knew French the following day.

'Well, okay,' I agreed, 'our French is fairly skin-deep. Perhaps we need intensive courses. You know the stuff – language laboratory, reinvention of texts, that kind of jazz. Will just arsing around France really improve our grasp of the language that much?'

Eoin laughed.

'Isn't that just exactly the name of the game? Listen, during this last year I have done lots of "*auto-stop*". That's what they call hitch-hiking, incidentally. You get into a car, and you talk, talk, talk, for maybe two or three hours. Perhaps the guy is lonely. You help to pass the time for him. They are keen to talk too. They tell you things that you might not know – seeing that you are a foreigner and all. Well, where would you get practice like that, the round of the year?'

'Perhaps you have a point,' I conceded. I was impressed.

Eoin paused a moment, seemed to hesitate, then continued. 'To be truthful – and perhaps this bit is just imagination – but I think that some of it is because I am a seminarian. They can pick us out, see. I don't know how – I don't wear any special clothes. One chap told me that he only takes seminarians and guys doing their military service: 'They're safe!' he said.

'Innocents abroad,' I mocked. 'They know you guys are all virgins.'

Eoin smiled.

'Well, maybe so, and maybe not. Actually, most of these fellows have not darkened the door of a church or a chapel in a hundred years, or never. But, at some level, there is a sort of nostalgia, or a search for something. Then, one day, they see a little man of God begging for a lift. So, I am poor and humble, probably a foreigner, not a threat. They feel superior to me, and they will never see me again – that's also a plus! Well just sometimes – but perhaps more often than you would think – in these very special circumstances, they cough it all up.'

'They cough what all up, Eoin?'

'Whatever they have lodged in their gut, Andrew. Amazing things. I'm not a priest yet, but these people are telling me totally private things, secrets, most often things that they had done, or things that they had had done to them during the war, terrible stuff that they have kept bottled up inside them ever since.'

'Sure, the war is a lifetime away, Eoin.'

'Yes, Andrew, exactly twenty-three years ago. That's a lifetime for you and for me. But someone who was forty, say, when the war ended, would still only be in his early sixties today. That is not really old.

Listen, the very first time I went to Paris, last Hallowe'en, a guy like that – early sixties – took me up after ten minutes. He drove me straight to Paris, then miles out of his way to Pontoise. The only time we stopped was for him to buy me a meal in a wayside restaurant. We talked non-stop. He was a Jew. He had lost everything and everyone in the extermination camps in Poland – wife, parents, children. He was the only one to walk out of there alive.'

'*Jesus!*' I punctuated with feeling.

'Well, I'll tell you another thing,' Eoin continued, 'that chap was one of the most beautiful people, one of the most generous, one of the most sensitive people I have ever met. But he found it impossible to believe in God after, well, after all the shit that had happened to him. He said to me two or three times, '*j'essaie de me garder propre*' I think he meant, 'I try to be a good person – to keep my integrity – but that's it.'

I can tell you, after a session like that, it would take me weeks to recover. Actually, I'm not the better of it yet. There are things that, once you hear them, you can never forget.'

'But you learnt French,' I interjected.

Eoin nodded his head slowly.

'You can say that again. It is burnt into your soul: words, phrases, intonations!'

I thought about Eoin's proposal for a few days. I could see that he would be brilliant at hitch-hiking. Light-boned for fitting neatly into cars, freckles on his freckles, always smiling, he would convince even the most suspicious of drivers at a hundred yards that he was as honest and good-natured as the day was long. Besides, if he was really God's roving ambassador, I thought, he obviously had an advantage: God would be sure to fix him up with some good lifts.

I had never hitch-hiked. As a result of anxious and, of course, impartial scrutiny in the bathroom mirror, my internal jury was cautiously satisfied that I didn't look too bad either. But Eoin had emphasised the importance of a winning smile, to encourage potential carriers to hit the brakes. I was much less good in the smiling department. Eoin always smiled at everybody. It was just his nature. He could be very funny about people, but never bitchy. He always took them at their best. My own trial-run smiles in the bathroom mirror were, frankly, an embarrassment. They looked ingratiating and insincere, like, 'Creep, can I use you and your pathetic banger to hitch a ride? Hee! Hee!' Too vomit-inducing, my internal jury decided harshly. 'If I was a driver, and I saw a smile like *that*,' I snarled at the mirror, 'I'd stand on the accelerator instead of on the brake!'

And yet, I did feel in my bones that I would be better off out of Strasbourg – sooner rather than later. The situation was deteriorating, and I felt no inclination to study. With regular work-patterns disrupted, and in an atmosphere of social and moral disintegration, it was a dangerous time for doing nothing. Nature abhors a vacuum – especially in the month of May. I could so easily end up regretting, at my leisure, what I had done when I was busy doing nothing.

To speak plainly, I had a short list of predatory females who, I suspected, probably also had me on their lists of predatory males. Birds and Bees Syndrome was kicking in, big time. All the symptoms were there, a textbook case! Maybe I would be safer and wiser wandering around France with Eoin, taking cold showers, exercising and absorbing French through my sweaty pores. I decided to go.

Eoin was happy. 'It will be like old times,' he said, and I knew what he meant.

He also had clear and exact ideas about how we should proceed.

'We travel separately, and we meet up every evening.'

'Travel separately!' I protested. 'Good Lord, why?'

'First of all, because you have to be alone with the driver to get a really decent conversation going. He has got to identify with you as somebody he likes talking to. Otherwise he'd just talk generalities to both of us, tourist-guide stuff.'

'That's okay with me. You can't expect every driver to go to bed with you – or even to go to confession.'

Eoin laughed.

'Well, if it's coffee-table chit-chat that you want, okay. But you'll never ever own a language until you get to talk with real people.'

That was Eoin. People did like to talk to him. He was a listener, a healing listener, even when he said nothing himself.

'There is another reason to travel separately,' Eoin said. 'Talk to drivers, and they will tell you straight up, 'When it comes to hitch-hikers, my policy is: one fellow or two girls.'

'Why?'

'It's obvious. With two guys, and one of them sitting behind the driver, they can overpower you, rob you, steal your car, use it for a bank robbery, a suicide bombing, or whatever.'

'Okay. And why two girls?'

'That's obvious too, if you think of it. If you are alone in a car with one girl, she could accuse you of anything – and, in fact, you might even try it on, too.'

'Holy Judas! Do you realise that the only reason why I'm coming with you on this caper is to try to avoid being alone with some bird for even five minutes any time for the next month?'

Eoin grinned and said nothing. But, like I said, he was a listener. When he did speak, he was serious.

'Hey, I suppose that things are not good, from that point of view – you know what I mean, psychologically, like – in student life, just at the moment.'

'No, you're damn right, things are falling apart. A few weeks of white-hot excitement – and then what? What next? What else? Nobody seems to know. The faculties are closed. The profs have already gone off to the Swiss Alps or wherever they go. People are suddenly waking up to the fact that, quite frankly, nobody cares what the students do between now and next October. It's like they have been on one ferocious piss-up, and now they've got one monumental collective hangover. They're demoralised and disillusioned. The situation out there is volatile and dangerous. Guys – and girls equally, I suppose – could land themselves into some very lousy situations – if they haven't already done so – through sheer frustration. I pity kids a few years younger than us. At least we've been around the block – well, I have anyhow.'

Eoin met my gaze. He nodded.

'In my own way, Andrew, in my own way.'

I never knew what he meant.

So, we travelled separately. We each had a rucksack, a sleeping bag, a thin foam mattress, wash things, a change of clothes, something to sleep in, a warm pull-over, swimming togs, maps, torches, an inflatable pillow, a plate, a mug, something to read – and Eoin's prayer-book! Our shared possessions consisted of a small ridge tent, a useful stove, some dry stores, a lamp, a radio, a first-aid kit, a saucepan, a kettle, basic cutlery, a pack of cards, soap powder and clothes pegs, because we expected to wash clothes at every campsite where we stayed! We did not have any furniture, though we did acquire a shabby but perfectly service-able folding stool from a skip at the first camping site where we spent a night. We distributed these communal belongings equi-tably between our two rucksacks, and always felt that we were travelling light.

We planned to eat fresh food, concentrating on one good meal in the evening. Both of us were quite good cooks, so we could hope to eat well: simple fare, but nutritious and cheap. Normally, on the road, we would travel in shorts – we both had the ones with cascading zips and pockets going everywhere and nowhere, indispensable, no doubt, for keeping clever things in for a rainy day out in the Kalahari Desert or up the Amazon Valley. In the cool of the evening, we would probably wear trousers.

We had brought, and indeed needed, an effective sunblock for Eoin, who was fair-skinned. I did not have to worry about the sun, having been told frequently by my darling mother that I look like a Sicilian bandit. She used to gaze at me and inquire wonderingly out loud, 'Where did I get you?', to which I could hardly be expected to have a ready reply.

We did not bring those annoying light plastic raincoats that were all the rage forty years ago. People were dazzled by the fact that they could fold up so small as to fit in the palm of your hand. But, in fact, their only function was to sluice every drop of water that fell straight onto your lower limbs and into your shoes and socks. If it rained, we said, we would prefer to get democratically wet, by which we meant, of course, equally wet all over.

Where were we going? Vaguely west, then south, then east, then north: a complete tour de France, if we ever got that far. We had arranged that either one or the other would telephone the old folks at home twice a week, to report where we were and how we were doing. As my parents knew Eoin's parents well, this was a good plan to keep everybody happy. In fact, forty years ago, before cellphones and e-mail forced everybody to make perfect nuisances of themselves, neither of us hardly ever called up home. A weekly letter in both directions was regarded as more than enough to reassure everyone that everybody loved everyone else. Besides, so long ago, making even a local call in a campsite was like trying to pick a lock.

CHAPTER THREE

We started our odyssey on Monday 3 June 1968. It was a fine morning, and, in fact, until it ceased to matter, we never saw rain. We were out on the road to Saverne at eight o'clock in the morning. In those days, before we caught the European disease, this used to be the middle of the night for any normal Irishman.

Traffic was brisk, as weekenders flooded westward ho! Eoin had thoughtfully agreed to let me go first, as he was a much more experienced hitch-hiker than me. Not to frighten off motorists who subscribed to the mantra of 'one guy or two girls', he concealed himself modestly behind the gable end of a garden shed to watch how I got on. After ten minutes, when I had caught nothing, he began to question my technique.

'Too hang-dog,' he called, 'too abject. Smile. Have fun. Look them in the eye. Don't be ashamed of what you're doing!'

The truth was that, if not actually ashamed, I was certainly embarrassed, and it showed. So I changed tack, adopting a non-chalant, back-hand gesture which seemed to say to drivers, 'I'm only doing this for your benefit, cretin, and I don't honestly give a shit whether you stop or not.'

My tutor was appalled: 'Andy, what are you doing!

To my great satisfaction, it was precisely at that moment that a car pulled up. When I was halfway into loading my rucksack onto the back seat, the driver spotted Eoin peeping out from behind his wall.

'Hey, what's this, another?' he asked suspiciously.

'No, no,' I reassured him with indecent haste, 'that's nothing. He's just the village idiot!'

We drove off.

That day, it took five cars, eight hours, and, in the end, public transport to get me to the *Camping Municipal* at Versailles. I arrived at about five o'clock in the afternoon. Meanwhile, Eoin, who had left Strasbourg after me, had soon found a driver who had brought him all the way to Versailles by three o'clock. I would not be surprised to hear that the same driver had bought him lunch, as well, and helped him to put up his tent when they arrived at the campsite. As I have said before – and will likely say again – Eoin was magic with people.

We had picked Versailles because it was west of Paris, and we were heading west, for Le Mont Saint-Michel, on the borders of Normandy and Brittany. Neither of us wanted to 'do' Paris, or even Versailles, in the context of a camping/hitch-hiking holiday. Our targets were villages and small towns with a campsite, a beach or a swimming pool, and an interesting chateau or monument nearby.

Meanwhile, though the facilities at the camping site in Versailles were good – for forty years ago, anyhow – it was already quite crowded. We would probably not have got in at all if Eoin had arrived any later in the day. In a few weeks' time, when the holiday season had got into full swing, it would most likely be strictly 'bookings only'. So, we had a real sense of achievement. In the very first day, we had taken Paris – indeed overrun it – and were securely dug in for the night.

We sat with our backs to two trees, and drank a celebratory beer. Then I had a hot shower. Eoin had taken his earlier. So, it was he who did the 'haute cuisine thing' that first night, with ingredients which he had bought at an open-air market. He had been lucky to find one still trading during the mid-afternoon. The results were: asparagus tips, lamb cutlets, fried potatoes, fresh celery, gateau de la Forêt-Noire, and coffee. Well up to my high standards.

We aimed at having three courses and coffee for those evening meals. It was a question of discipline and pride for us, when we were tired at the end of the day, not to act the slob and eat trash food. The first and third courses, it was agreed, would usually be cold, because we only had one stove and a kettle. For starters, we could have cold fish, asparagus, avocado, terrine, or pâté with interesting side salads. For dessert, the choice was extensive: ice cream, fruit, yogurt, or anything from the delicious range of French patisseries. For the main course, it would be meat, chicken, fish, with fresh vegetables, and, as Irishmen, almost mandatory potatoes.

Regrettably, Eoin introduced rice on one or two occasions. My attitude to rice was that – quite apart from the fact that I don't particularly like the stuff – we are probably going to be living under Chinese rule for quite long enough. Monsieur Alain Peyrefitte, who featured earlier on in this story as the ill-starred minister for education, later wrote a book entitled *Quand La Chine S'éveillera*, meaning: when China wakes up –

which frightened the pants off me.

After supper, we strolled over to the campsite bistro and had another beer. We got chatting with three girls, of more or less the same age as ourselves. They were French Canadians, as we soon discovered from their distinctive accent, vocabulary, and syntax. Besides, even nowadays, you don't often see French girls on their own in campsites or bistros. These Canadian birds – as we would have called them in those days when we didn't know any better – were lively, pretty, and just as opinionated as ourselves. In Dublin dialect, they were good gas. We enjoyed ourselves.

Back in the tent, when we had turned in for the night, we were chatting in the dark about one thing and another. I suddenly said to Eoin – à propos of nothing at all, 'Eoin, are you not fond of *les girls*?'

There was a silence. I thought at once that I should not have asked him that, and that he was offended. But, after a pause, he said, 'Are you really asking me, am I fond of *les mecs* instead?'

He meant, of course, boys. I was stunned at his directness, and at the thought that this was precisely what I was asking him.

'God, no, Eoin,' I exclaimed, half-lying, 'I didn't mean it that way. Like, I've known you all my life, and I've never got that vibe off you.'

Then I added – in a hole, and still digging furiously – 'But, if you are, I mean, like, that way, you know, it doesn't bother me at all – you're still my friend.'

There was another silence. If the roles were reversed, I scolded myself, I could not imagine Eoin being so utterly clueless. But when he spoke again, there was no anger, or even tension, in his voice. He said, very quietly – and it was certainly the reply that I deserved: 'Don't worry, Andrew. There's no way I'll be jumping up on you in the middle of the night.'

I laughed uneasily, then rushed to say something compromising about myself, so that he would not feel that it was only *his* sexuality that was fair game for this inquisition that I had somehow managed to unleash.

'Look, Eoin, I'm not exactly an angel myself. But I am not Europe's number one stud either. I have had a few adventures – most of them absolute disasters. What is positive, I think, is that I *do* want to be in love, I *do* want to get married, and I *do* want to have children, and to be faithful to the woman I love – all that jazz.

'So this is what I am really asking you: how does the sex thing work for you? Do you not really want someone to love, to marry? I'm not asking you out of vulgar curiosity, but . . . because – well, because I've known you forever and you are really a person whom I like and respect.'

'Okay, Andy, that is very honest, so I will level with you too. I have never slept with a girl. I have never slept with a boy either. Technically – if that is the word – I am a virgin, at least in fact, if not always in desire. To be honest, there are times when this makes no sense at all for me. Sometimes I am desperate, and abject. I can even revert to the stuff we did when we were kids, and I am ashamed.

There is a phrase in the Gospel that I hold on to, "The Son of Man has nowhere to lay his head." That means – for me anyhow – he has no lips, no breast where he can lay his head. That is my situation too. It's not just a little rule or regulation of the Holy Roman Church. People who say that simply don't know what they're talking about. Heaven itself has destined no sweetheart for me. I am certain of that. I admit that I don't really understand it. I resent it sometimes, and I do experience it as a – what's the word? – a diminishment. Yes. And yet, I know that Christ has called to me: "Follow Me." I just have to grow into that vocation.'

'Well, that's very noble – even beautiful, in its own way. But let's be real, Eoin. What about infatuation? What about when you just cannot help yourself?'

He thought for a while. Then he said: 'Stendhal has this theory about what he calls "*la cristallisation affective*". It means that we don't fall in love unless we want to. If I feel called to give my life to God, it doesn't mean that I become insensitive to other people. On the contrary, I am doing it *for* those other people as well. It's important for all of us to each be what we were meant to be. What it *does* mean, is that I have to do whatever it takes to avoid this "crystillisation of the affections". Because, in my case, that would always be selfish.

'Is that hard?'

'Not really, for people who are wholly generous. So that's what I have to work on. And, yes, *that* is sometimes hard.'

I thought about what I should say, something encouraging but not patronising. In the end, I settled for: 'Hey Eoin! You're not doing so bad, huh?'

He did not reply, but, in the dark, I sensed that he was smiling. I heard him yawn once or twice, then he turned on his side, and soon I was listening to the gentle rhythm of his breathing. He was asleep.

I lay for a long while, my hands behind my head, reflecting on what he had said. I realised that I would have listened to very few people saying such things, without thinking that they were either fools or out-and-out hypocrites. For Eoin, I wanted what he had said to be true – even if I could not make head nor tail of it.

The good die young, they say. Is that why? Is it perhaps that even God would be ashamed to allow such a good person to find out what life is really like. From that night onwards, I had a sort premonition, a fear. I knew that Eoin was terribly vulnerable.

CHAPTER FOUR

In 1968, cell phones were probably no more than a gleam in some nutty professor's eye. I suppose the Kremlin and Pentagon had cumbersome prototypes as bulky as cadillacs, but they were certainly not available to the great unwashed worldwide. No harm either. Cell phones, or mobiles, are as addictive as nicotine: a new and reprehensible form of oral gratification. Think of the long journeys by public transport where one cannot read, think, or sleep, because one's neighbours are rabbiting away about their incredibly boring lives, loves, or dismal employments. I am told that in Germany, you can't do it in public. Well, good for the Germans!

All that being said, we would have had many uses for mobile phones to coordinate our manoeuvres during the following weeks. For instance, starting from the outskirts of Versailles, that second day, Eoin managed to maintain an apprroximately straight course along the N12 to Le Mont Saint-Michel, passing through Dreux, Alençon, Mayenne, and Fougères. Meanwhile I veered wildly north, via the N13 through Evreux, to Caen. At first, I thought I was doing famously, because I had got one fast car to take me the whole way to Caen. But then my sorrows began.

Eoin had forgotten to instruct me on one further and vital item of hitch-hiker's technique. This was, that if your driver is finishing his journey in a city or large town – and if you want to go further – get out of that car *before* the urban sprawl. This was essential in the days before most big towns had ring roads around them. Experienced drivers, in those days, who saw you thumbing a lift on the outskirts of a big town that they were approaching, would know that you wanted to continue your journey beyond it, and would be sympathetic, knowing that your only alternative was to foot-slog your way, rucksack on shoulder, right across the concrete jungle.

That is exactly what I had to do in Caen. Besides, half the way through, I was bursting for a leak. That always happens to me, when I can't have one. I won't say where I leaked eventually, except to confess that this was a sacrilegious one. William the Conqueror – appropriately abbreviated as 'W.C.' – had filled the city of Caen with pious monuments, as far back as the eleventh century. I was certainly in angelic company when I did what angels never have to do.

William the Conqueror is actually called 'William the Bastard' in France. The English don't tell you that, of course. It probably proves that the French discovered Australia in the Dark Ages – just like the Chinese are reputed to have really found America in 1421 – a full seventy years before Christopher Columbus. My reason for advancing this daring theory is that, to this day, Australians regard 'bastard' as a term of affectionate commiseration.

Caen was bombed to bits in the last year of the second world war, as the Allied forces smashed their way from the landing beaches of the Cherbourg peninsula towards Paris, and, ultimately, the whole way to Berlin. The city had to be substantially rebuilt after the war. The rule about post-war rebuilding is sadly, but almost invariably, followed: the first is the worst. Perhaps I was not seeing Caen at its best. Caen was certainly not seeing me at *my* best. I was hot, hungry, tired, in bad need of a leak, and convinced that nobody loved me – until William the Bastard came to my rescue.

The afternoon was slow torture – all towns beginning with 'V', Villers-Bocage, Vassy, Vire, Villedieu-les-Poêles – where motorists gave me cheery waves and did not stop. They seemed to have a special wave in this *Basse Normandie* – not quite the 'V for victory' sign, but its first cousin, the two fingers – with unmistakable overtones of sadism. Of course, I had quickly forgotten the first rule of the game, as patiently explained by my gentle teacher: smile. My beetroot scowl and voluble body-language were bellowing in all possible registers, 'Stop, *please*, so that I can strangle you!'

I walked the whole way from Pontaubault to Mont Saint-Michel by the coast road, a distance of at least ten miles. More than one carload of happy holiday-makers, bewitched by the spectacular silhouette of the Mont, which could be seen on the horizon from miles away, nearly tumbled me into the ditch. According to my computer, Le Mont Saint-Michel is number four on the list of 'The Seven Forgotten Wonders of the Medieval Mind'. Big deal! Even if I had known this forty years ago – it would have cut no ice with me. Why! Even the seven *real* wonders of the world would always have taken second place to my own precious ass. I cursed those idiot drivers fluently. They waved enthusiasticaly back – and did not stop.

I did see one thing to cheer me up, in the murderous frame of mind that had descended on me. It was a scene straight out of Brueghel – or perhaps Hieronymus Bosch in a skittish humour. I had just toiled up a hill, rucksack straps cutting cruelly into my armpits, causing me to excrete, from irritated pores, skunk-like odours, odious even to myself.

A fat peasant woman had embarked on the ascent after me, and was heaving her way upwards, exuding from her person, I don't doubt, all the perfumes of Arabia. She was laden, not with a rucksack, but with one of these outlandish shoulder harnesses – a bucket hanging down on either side of her, like a surrealist scales of justice. I could scarcely believe it. I would have thought that such contraptions had gone out of fashion around the time of the Black Death.

Meanwhile, the third horseman of the Apocalypse, in the shape of a youth aged about fifteen, had also engaged with the hill, and was labouring up it on a racing bicycle with dropped handlebars. Totally absorbed in his dream of winning the Tour de France when his legs had got a little longer, this lad was straining every muscle in his slight body. Standing on the pedals, his head was about level with his knees. Unless he had eyes in his backside, which was about the most forward part of his anatomy, he had to be wholly unsighted.

I confess that I saw it coming, and I did nothing to prevent it. There are situations where one is as if paralysed – hypnotised – by the ghastly inevitability of what is about to happen. As Anouilh so truly says, '*c'est reposant, la tragédie!*' In the presence of pure comedy or true tragedy, we don't really have to do anything. And this was both.

WHAM! No smart bomb could be smarter. Right on target,

to the nether and hinder cleavage of *Madame la Paysanne*. In an instant, boy, bicycle, buckets, buxom beauty, and harness were rolling wantonly together in the bushes. I stood idly by, not knowing what might be required of me in such a situation. A soothing body-count might be the best option, and the safest outcome, from my point of view. I sensed that, if there were survivors from the collision, violent hostilities might be about to break out. Cravenly, I feared that I might be caught in the crossfire or even obliged to take sides.

When the *dramatis personae* had sorted out their respective body parts, the woman hit the boy with an enormous clatter across the cheek, following it up with a left hook that would have floored Muhammad Ali. She, for one, was definitely firing on all cylinders. I was not so sure about the child, who had blood on his face and looked quite dazed. When he found his tongue, he began to stammer apologies in words so humble and so obviously sincere that she was completely won over. She was last seen crushing the poor boy to death in a remorseless embrace, and clucking like a hen about *his* injuries. Two is company. I went on my way.

I don't know what the dynamics of this burlesque scene were. Its effect on me was to realise that both woman and boy were nice people, and were, each in their own way, better than myself, who had been in a self-centred sulk all afternoon. Instead of getting even further depressed – as I would have done routinely in those days, whenever I realised that yet another person was less of a pain in the bum than myself – I cheered up immediately, and stayed in good humour for the rest of the day. This was a new experience for me. Perhaps, after all, I was on the road to somewhere?

The D275 ends up at a T-junction at the start of the isthmus, going due north to the base of Mont Saint-Michel. At least, that is the way it was in those days. There are probably half a dozen flyovers now, and a six-lane auto-route plunging straight into the Atlantic. In our innocence, we had thought that there would be only one campsite in the neighbourhood. In fact, even then, there were at least four or five. Eoin had installed himself at a pleasant site north of Beauvoir, a mile or two from the Mont. By luck more than skill, I had little trouble finding him.

After a shower and a beer, I had completely recovered from the hardships of my journey. Indeed, I was already beginning to feel proud of being an authentic *auto-stoppeur*. I had certainly been blooded as such – if not actually bloodied. During supper we told each other our adventures of the day.

Eoin had been wafted the whole way to Alençon by an auxiliary bishop of somewhere, wearing all his ceremonial feathers – or rather, by the prelate's gloomy driver. The bishop occupied the entire back seat of the car, and Eoin was invited to sit beside the driver as a sort of postillion. Unlike so many of Eoin's fellow-travellers, the bishop did not talk about his soul to a mere seminarian. Instead, he questioned Eoin closely about his seminary regime – obviously to see if it was sufficiently fuddy-duddy for that prelate's liking. Eoin's comments were uncharacteristically caustic.

'He was really quite invasive, if that's the right word. I mean, very nosy. He was literally pumping me for information – about our timetable, whether we could go out in the evenings, what permissions did we need to get, were we allowed to associate with girls, were there restrictions on what we were permitted to read, did we have to have a named and approved spiritual director – even how often we were "required" to go to confession! I had the impression that he would not hesitate to use any tittle-tattle that I gave him to make trouble for anyone he regarded as too liberal. I was careful not to tell him about Père Ou. He would hate like hell to hear about him!'

Eoin was the most tolerant of people, someone who treated almost anyone – from crabbed conservative to lunatic-fringe liberal – with respect. So, his tone about this bishop quite surprised me. It was definitely not just an act put on for my benefit – to show that Eoin was still one of the lads, and not a complete Holy Mary. I was intrigued. What could make him so sharp, so *intolerant*?

I worked it out later. The one thing that Eoin could not abide was mean-mindedness. It annoyed him that this peacock was using his rank, and the fact that he was giving a snot-nosed seminarian a free ride in his car, to over-awe him into being indiscreet and disloyal to people whom he respected, and who had made him welcome in Strasbourg. In Eoin's book, that was squalid and mean-minded.

He continued, 'Meanwhile, I was stealing sidelong glances at the driver, who was a young priest, only a few years older than ourselves. He was practically wincing – realising perfectly well what was going on, hating it all, and knowing that it was just abject and wrong. Poor beggar! I don't think he uttered a single word during the entire journey. Perhaps he was not allowed to. Six months driving a dinosaur like that round the place would do anybody's head in.'

The bishop, it seems, went on to be scathing about the Student Revolution. He kept calling it names like 'insolence' or 'insubordination' or – his favourite – '*effronterie*'. He clearly had a bleakly hierarchical view of the world, with people like himself sitting firmly on top of the pile, while the rest of us, by divine decree, squirmed beneath their fat bottoms.

The truth, I suppose, is that – for all their ballyhoo – the French are not really any good at revolutions. Witness, for example, the French Revolution, which quickly spiralled down into the obscenity of the Terror. You could add 1832, 1848, 1870 – each a disaster in its own way. But the absolute contempt that this bishop was expressing for the students and their motives was totally wrong-headed. Eoin and I both knew people who had committed themselves to the revolution, for the most idealistic and unselfish of reasons.

I said to Eoin, 'Your pal in the purple feathers is furious, because he knows that the tumbrils are rumbling out for him, and for his kind.'

'What do you mean?'

'It figures,' I replied. 'He asks you all those nosy-parker questions about the seminaries, and then he starts into a tirade against the students. That means he knows full well that, if this stupid revolution never produces anything else, it will still blow his kind of seminary right out of the water.'

I added unwisely – and I suppose unfairly – 'The kind of seminary where mice are trained to be rats, like himself.'

Eoin coloured at that, but contented himself with saying quietly, 'Hey, that's a bit rough, isn't it?'

To change the subject rapidly, I launched into a wildly exaggerated description of my own day. Like a true Irishman hearing a story from another Irishman, Eoin knew exactly how much to believe and how much to enjoy. I can be very funny describing my own deep sorrows – which is not an entirely admirable trait in my character. It is, in fact, my sly way of rewriting history – as something hilarious, instead of as something that had reduced me to a vicious temper and a craven sulk. The retake tends to be much more attractive than the raw material – which can be very raw indeed. It's the way you tell it, of course. Art-forms can gift-wrap the most ferocious lies. It happens all the time in autobiographies, of course.

After supper, we did a quick once-over of the Mont, in the company of a French chap and his girl, with whom we had palled up at the camp site. I forget his name. He was eminently forgettable, anyhow. She was called Marieke, after the song by Jacques Brel, whom we all hero-worshipped at the time. She was lovely, and absolutely wasted on that yokel. Love is blind, whereas jealousy has 20/20 vision.

The next day, we spent several hours on the Mont. This is not a tourist-guide, so I can be as impressionistic and inaccurate as I like. Besides, I do not need to describe Le Mont, because it must be one of the most recognisable landscapes in the world. From the point of view of the photographer, the painter, the architect, or the poet, it is an indescribably exquisite, and har-monious, composition. In the less soulful perspective of the geographer or the topographer, the Mount is merely another '*presqu'île*'. But the French love *presqu'îles*. The country is full of them. *Presqu'île* is merely a literal translation of the Latin, *pene insula*, peninsula: almost-an-island.

Everybody knows that you are not meant to approach the Mont except by the approved causeway. That is because, across what you think are vast expanses of flat and harmless sand, the tide will suddenly rush in from America or wherever, 'at the speed of wild horses', as all the best guidebooks say. That will be the highest tide you have ever seen in your whole life – and, likely, the last tide that you'll ever see. In next to no time, you'll be soaked to the skin, and dead.

If, by some unbelievable fluke, you avoid being dead because of the tide, you will certainly be dead because of the shifting sands in the Bay of Mont Saint-Michel. They are all over the place, it seems, and 'treacherous' is the favourite word guidebooks use to describe them. They will not hesitate to suck you down to your doom, but slowly – like a python swallowing a donkey. He takes his time. But he does get it done in the end.

The year previous to coming to Strasbourg, I had read all ten volumes of *Les Misérables* in French, as a sort of linguistic and cultural initiation. Somewhere in there, Victor Hugo minutely describes somebody being clawed down, millimetre by millimetre, by shifting sands. This is not in the musical version – much too slow for that – but it must be one of the most horrifying things that I have ever read.

So much for the in-depth topography, and I'll skip most of the history. What I could call 'the present phase' seems to begin in the year 966, when Richard I, Duke of Normandy, installed a Benedictine monastery on top of the Mont, where it has been performing a balancing act, more or less successfully, ever since. Once, when the monks were all in bed, half the church toppled over the north-facing cliff into the sea. Another night, when the monks were saying their prayers in the church, it was the dormitory's turn to disappear over the brink. St Benedict, Eoin told me, was a stickler for being in the right place at the right time. He had a point, hadn't he?

The Mont became strategically important in the fourteenth century, when the Hundred Years War – whatever that was about – was going on. So, the French built mighty ramparts on the south side of the *presqu'île*, from which they flung all kinds of unpleasant items down on the English, thereby making the abbey, and the village clutching to its coat-tails, almost impregnable. Besides, the Archangel Michael, who presides spectacularly over the whole bay, has a serious reputation as an intergalactic warrior, largely thanks to the Book of the Apocalypse. After about thirty years, the English got depressed, and went back home to Piccadilly Circus, where all that they had learned from their various experiences in Europe eventually expressed itself in a compromise statue between St Michael on the Mont and the Manikin-Piss dolly-boy in Brussels.

Graham Robb, in his interesting book *The Discovery of France*, says that 'Mont Saint-Michel was already crammed with bars and souvenir shops in the eighteenth century.' If so, it was very unusual, because the tourist trade did not really exist until a hundred years later. It is estimated that, nowadays, three million people visit the Mont every year. That means an average of ten thousand a day, with many more at peak periods. Where do they all fit? As we discovered, there is only one narrow street, optimistically called La Grande Rue, which snakes up to the monastery at the summit. There are also paths along the ramparts and from the less-used Porte Eschaugette – all on the south side of the *presqu'île*. The 'plain people' have no access to the entire north side of the Mont.

The abbey became a prison during the French Revolution and Empire, and was in need of extensive restoration by the end of the nineteenth century. The monks moved back in 1966 for the celebration of the thousandth anniversary of the founding of the abbey – and in nice time for Eoin to get Mass there at midday, which, of course, pleased him greatly. I even came with him. Eoin did not doubt that Divine Providence had arranged everything for his own convenience. Indeed, he seemed to believe this always, whether the news was superficially good or bad. If it is true that a man dies as he lives, this reassures me a little about Eoin's last moments. He will have thought surely that even his death was a brilliant idea.

CHAPTER FIVE

Is Mont Saint-Michel in Normandy or in Brittany? The diplomatic answer is that it is where the one meets the other. On the following day, we travelled west, unambiguously into Brittany. We followed the coast road, and, knowing that progress would be slow – these were relatively minor roads, and most cars travelling them seemed to be going no further than the nearest beach – we decided to travel together, and not to worry about covering enormous distances. We did a lot of walking that day, but the sea breeze kept us cool, and as we strode along in step, we sang every song that we knew, and even more that we didn't know at all. We were happy – and people must have got a good vibe from us. They smiled and waved, and some of them even offered us lifts. We did have a bit of hassle getting through Saint-Brieuc, but we ended up by mid-afternoon in an absolutely perfect camping site at Saint-Quay-Portrieux. This became our headquarters for the next few days.

Built in grassy terraces above a golden beach, the campsite was strikingly lovely. And yet, most campers and caravan-owners were cautious about installing themselves too far forward, overhanging the sea. In such an exposed position, they – and we also – could have been in serious trouble, if a sudden squall blew up from any point of the compass. Being young and foolish, we took the gamble, and it came off.

For those two or three days, we unwound, physically and psychologically, from the stresses and strains of the past year. We did always have to work that bit harder, because our grasp of French, though quite good, was by no means perfect. Also, it was only when we began to relax that we realised how tensed up we had been since the Student Revolution had begun. And, most particularly, I was having a delicious holiday from what I shall call euphemistically my 'emotional' life – meaning that I did not think of sex once during those dozen or so magical days at the beginning of June 1968. It seemed to me that this had not happened since I was about thirteen. Was it a good thing? Well, at least – without taking sides on that larger issue – I suppose that all preoccupations, and certainly all obsessions, can become burdensome. I was certainly due time off from that particular one.

So, what did we do? No doubt, there is nothing so boring to read about as precisely nothing at all – and that is exactly what we did do. Lazing around, sunbathing, reading our blockbusters, having five or six swims a day in lukewarm water, sauntering down town to do some desultory shopping, and finding the local people very friendly and all up for a chat. I left Eoin to pray for the two of us. He was very quiet at times, when I felt he must be talking to the boss. I sensed I should not interrupt. We did not drink until evening, when we had one or two beers in a bistro while playing darts, or possibly boules, with some senior citizens. At one stage, the golden oldies declared that we had, quite inadvertently, won at boules, and insisted on standing us some fire-water, by a name that sounded like shoe-shine. Based on honey, it is a local brew and – with no disrespect intended – likely to remain local, for the foreseeable future.

Later, in the bistro, people were interested to hear that we were students from Strasbourg, which most of them seemed to think was somewhere east of the North Pole. One old gentleman was quite convinced that Strasbourg – and indeed all of Alsace – was still in Germany, and that this accounted for our funny accents. When we said that we were from Ireland, we were greeted even more warmly as Celtic cousins, who – somewhat to our dismay – had to be treated to even more shoe-shine, and also to renditions on the *cornemuse*, which is a Breton bagpipes, even more nerve-jangling – if that is possible – than the Irish equivalent. No wonder that, in warfare, when the Celts wheel out this secret weapon, enemies tremble at the knees, and change their minds about whatever they had been planning to do in the line of aggression.

Next, we moved on to the topic of comparative philology. My own grasp of the Irish language was enough to pass the compulsory examinations, but I was never very fluent. Nevertheless, I enjoyed the conversation, and I still remember some of the striking similarities between Irish and the Breton language which we discovered that evening, so many years ago.

When it came to discussing the student revolution, most people smiled indulgently and seemed to think that the current eruptions were something the students would grow out of, like acne or dandruff. They shook their heads and said compassionately, '*Ah, les pauvres jeunes!*', without ever saying precisely why the students – or we ourselves, as some of those students – deserved to be pitied. I could not help contrasting their attitude with that of Eoin's bleak bishop, with his talk of insubordination and *effronterie*. I would be prepared to bet that none of these simple folk had ever been to university. They were, on the one hand, much more remote from that world than the pompous prelate. On the other, they were much nearer the truth of our situation, through simple empathy.

Finally, Eoin danced a jig for them, and – to uproarious applause – another. We had no music, but these Bretons accompanied the dance spontaneously with perfectly rhythmical hand-clapping and whooping at all the right places. Eoin was an absolute star. They loved him, not least because he so obviously wanted to please them and make them happy.

That night was sultry. We slept in the open air, '*sous la belle étoile*', with the sighing of the silvery sea for lullaby. I got a bit cold around dawn, and withdrew to the tent. Eoin never stirred until half past nine in the morning.

Even in those far-off days, I had plenty of experience of living in a tent. Before and all during my teen years, I had been a scout. Later on, with my wife, and then with our children, and now with our grandchildren – God bless them – we have been a family of enthusiastic campers.

Nowadays, my wife and I cheat ever so slightly, having bought ourselves a comfortable caravan. At our age, we have both had medical and surgical adventures, so do have to be a little more careful.

I still hanker for the days when I could sleep happily on the good earth – from which we have all come, and to which we shall one day all return. This will probably surprise you, but I think that it is easier to accept death – whether your own death or that of someone you have loved – if you have both slept from time to time '*par terre*'. I think of Eoin a lot every time I camp. It has been forty years. But when I wake up in the middle of the night in a tent – or even in a caravan – I still feel that, if I stretched out my hand in the dark, I could almost touch him.

Our thoughts when we left Saint-Quay-Portrieux were to zig-zag haphazardly through Brittany, where neither of us had ever been before. Our first impressions of our fellow Celts had been very positive; we were eager to prolong the experience. So, when we met somebody in the bistro on our last night who said he was driving to Saint-Brieuc the following day, we asked if we could come with him. The bad news was that he was leaving at half past six in the morning.

By some miracle, we were up and ready when our kindly chauffeur called to collect us in front of the campsite. I am afraid that we can hardly have been pleasant company for him, as we yawned, belched, farted, and hawked in response to his polite efforts at agreeable conversation. I have to say that, for a person so spiritual and indeed so refined as Eoin, he was reassuringly physical in the mornings – which was fine in the great outdoors, but a bit of a damper on happy chit-chat in the confines of an already overloaded '*deux-chevaux*'.

We breakfasted on the terrace of an early-bird café on the Place du Chai, at Saint-Brieuc, after which we felt a little more like some of the higher hominoids. A look around town did not reveal anything very memorable. In fairness to Saint-Brieuc, it is more noted for atmosphere than for architecture – and especially renowned for the liveliness of its musical and artistic scene in summer. That morning – as neither musicians nor artists are conspicuously noted as early risers – we obviously missed the best part.

When the tourist office opened, an ample lady with a single surprising pigtail advised us to visit Huelgoat, which she described as '*tout ce qu'il y a de délicieux*'. We hitched a ride in the back of a lorry, driven by a man whose language – or even the family of his language – we were quite unable to identitfy. We arrived in Huelgoat by about noon, and immediately decided to stay.

What a truly 'delicious' little town indeed! Huelgoat had probably fewer than two thousand citizens – in those days at least – though English retirees had already begun to find it and settle there. The name Huelgoat means the 'High Forest', and probably dates back to the age of Astérix and the Romans, when most of Brittany was densely wooded. The campsite was not crowded so early in the season. It was, and still is, presumably, on the banks of a scenic lake, which looks like an integral part of the natural landscape. In fact, that lake was created artificially in the sixteenth century to supply water for silver and lead mines in the vicinity. Not surprisingly, the river feeding the lake is called the Argent. This, of course, is the French for both 'silver' and 'money' – from the mythical days when each of those commodities was also the other.

Huelgoat was full of charming surprises. Right in the centre of the town is a literally enchanted forest, which is surely Huelgoat's most 'delicious' attraction. The River Argent winds its way between and around lovely trees, through pools, over and under boulders, disappearing and appearing again within a chaos of caves and grottos, each more magical than the last. The Rock Chaos, the Devil's Cave, King Arthur's Camp, and the Trembling Rock, which is an enormous boulder, weighing 137 tonnes, and yet can be got to shiver and shake by applying even moderate pressure. There was also a Forest Amphitheatre, where we both performed spontaneously. Fortunately – or certainly hopefully – there was no one in the audience to see or hear us.

In the bistro that night, in the company of two girls whose nationality I will not reveal, because they did something mean to us, we learned some more French vocabulary pertaining to beer. '*Un demi*' was a glass or a bottle of the magic potion – I knew that much. '*Un demi pression*' was a glass of draught beer. '*Un sérieux*' was a pint, or, I suppose, a half-litre of the stuff, whereas '*un formidable*' is an immoderate and unreasonable quantity of beer that nobody in their right senses would order to drink solo. So, we ordered *un formidable*, with the tacit agreement that all four of us would help to liquidate the liqour.

A glass jackboot was produced, containing possibly two litres of beer. It was manageable – just about. Speaking for myself, if I drink a pint and a half of beer, physiology kicks in. I have to go to the loo for the rest of the evening. Indeed, I have often had cause to be grateful to heaven for this trip-switch mechanism, which keeps me reasonably sober during marathon sessions. I cannot figure out people who drink six or seven pints on the trot, without ever having to visit the little boys' room. Where do they put all that beer? Probably where their brain is supposed to be!

On this occasion, all went well at first. I noticed with satisfaction that the girls were no slouches when it came to ingurgitating their share of the beer. Disaster befell us, though, when we turned the corner between the vertical of the leg and the horizontal of the foot in the glass jackboot. Marie – I think that was her name – had the boot to her head at that precise moment. Some pocket of air must have been released between the ankle and the upper, causing a tidal wave of fizzy beer to slap the lady in the face, flooding into her eyes, her mouth, and particularly her nose. She dropped the jackboot, which shattered to a thousand pieces on the flagged floor. We knew at once that we would have to pay for that glass – and, in the event, it did not come cheap.

Meanwhile, Marie was literally drowning in beer. She could not breathe, was purple in the face, and making horrible noises. We slapped her on the back. Her companion slapped her on the front. She got progressively worse, then vomited violently. At the very least, her last three meals came up. By now, everybody in the bistro was having the time of their lives. Two other girls were holding their mouths, as if they were about to come out in sympathy with Marie. Our little group was the centre and focus of disgusted attention.

The soirée ended badly. When Marie had at last got her speech back, she – with her companion's spontaneous support – decided to make a scene. You can see it from their point of view, of course. Nice girls did not then vomit in public – especially if the vomit was drink-related.

The girls stalked out, without even saying goodbye to us or to anyone. As well as being embarrassed by Marie's gala performance, I guess they did not want to clean up the mess, or to pay for the glass jackboot – both of which the management clearly expected our group to do. Eoin and I had to do it all instead. I could see some of the customers, and even the barman, stealing compassionate glances at us as – on our hands and knees – as we scraped up the gunge, and then emptied our pockets. Nobody said anything; we had broken a solemn taboo. Once a scapegoat had been found for such a crass reminder of human misery as vomit in a sacred space consecrated to conviviality, nobody wanted to know us. And nobody said '*Au revoir*' or '*Merci*' when we were leaving.

Eoin informed me on our way back to the campsite, that it was the same story with the original scapegoat in the Bible. A decent, respectable, God-fearing goat, he was driven out into the wilderness loaded with other people's sins.

'He was only a goat, see?' Eoin explained.

He added as an after-thought, 'I think that animals will get justice in the next life for all the things we have done to them.'

Eoin did have some pretty odd ideas.

In the tent that night, we discussed physicality, by which I don't mean sex. This time, we were moving on to important issues, like vomit, sweating, scratching, burping, and farts. I told Eoin that he was at his most physical in the morning, whereas I was most likely to get physical at night. He laughed. Then he asked me if I knew where the word 'humility' comes from. I replied that I hadn't a clue. So he said that it comes from 'humus', the good earth. In a sense, humility means to be earthy, to have your base – your feet – on the ground. He quoted a saying of one of those old Desert Fathers, 'He who is humble lies on the ground – Where can he fall to?' He added, 'Such a person is the ultimate realist.'

Eoin was like Père Ou. He could make spirituality out of anything – I mean real spirituality – not the usual pious claptrap.

We spent the next few days meandering around Brittany, sometimes splitting up for the road, but often travelling together. The Bretons did not seem to have heard about the 'one fellow, or two girls' rule, or perhaps they were just more laid back and trusting than the non-Celtic French. We saw – I cannot quite remember in what precise order – Locronan, the Camaret peninsula, Quimper, Concarneau, and Quiberon – yet another other *presqu'île*.

On our last night in Quiberon, we discussed, over un *demi pression*, where we had come from and where we wanted to go next. Like most people who live well up towards the Arctic Circle, our gut instinct, starting off, had been to move south as quickly as possible. Now, we decided to halt the helter-skelter lunge for the Equator, and to turn east into the Loire Valley. Eoin said, 'We might even buy one of dem chateaux,' jokingly pronouncing the 'x'.

Later that night – camping high above the sea, the sky beautifully cool and clear – we had left the doors of the tent wide open. Eoin was sound asleep. The deep silence seemed enhanced by his gentle breathing – in perfect counterpoint with the sighing of the sea. Thoughts formed that I fashioned and forged into words in the morning. They have been important to me over the years. In a strange way – that I cannot explain – by some sort of spiritual telepathy, they have always seemed like Eoin's legacy to me, his message.

'Our tent is a place where we are one with Creation. It is a living membrane, stirring with the wind, pulsating with the earth, trembling, fragile, and beautiful. In the deep silence of this night, our little tent opens upon the measureless beauty of the sea, and the stars, and of the whole vast universe. We are infinitely vulnerable – and infinitely secure.'

CHAPTER SIX

We went east towards the Loire, and ended up well north of the river, at a place called Laval. The reasoning behind this was that we had been told by someone that the most interesting chateaux were to be found 'before the river turns south'. This was an impressively assertive, if not downright inaccurate, piece of information.

We had split up again for the hitch-hiking, each making his own way. I regarded myself as, by now, initiated into the mysteries of auto-stopping. This meant that I found it easier to smile at drivers, not lose my cool, and not to fly into a fury or stage a full-blown endogenous depression every time I had to be a little bit patient. I told myself, in a knowing and superior way, that such excessive reactions indicated that I had been pathetically insecure, whereas I was now, thankfully, full of wisdom and maturity.

Heading out of Quiberon, I got a chap who drove me the whole way to Redon, or almost the whole way – and thereby hangs a tale. This guy was pretty weird. His conversation, which came in fits and starts, consisted of a bewildering succession of perorations and non-sequiturs, delivered with considerable vehemence, but, apparently – and very conveniently – not requiring any particular response from the audience, which at the time numbered only myself. Knowing as much as I do now about these things, I would say that the lad was as high as a kite on drugs.

A few miles from Redon, my chauffeur swung abruptly left, off the main road, and plunged with his by-now-familiar vindictiveness up a forest road, leading to precisely nowhere. This, emphatically, was not part of the contract. Alarmed, I tried to demur, to question, to urge, to suggest, to reason and, finally, to protest. Deaf ears! The guy was completely impervious and impenetrable. He was also a big and powerful man. It came to me with a hideous jolt that I was a weakling in comparison, and only too pervious and penetrable, and completely at his mercy. I panicked. Rape, robbery, and murder seemed to be on the agenda – in whichever order, and perhaps simultaneously.

It got worse.

My prospective and imminent nemesis then lurched off even the forest track that he had been following, and bumped his way over roots of trees into a clearing, where he came to a juddering halt. There was the silence of after-shock in that car for several pregnant seconds. Pregnant with what? That was the question. Contrary to my fears and expectations, my off-the-wall driver, it seemed, had no plans to rape, rob, or kill me. He simply folded his hands on the steering-wheel, bent his head down on his clasped palms, and fell fast asleep. To my amazement, I was, for a split-second, not so much relieved as curiously peeved that my presence and possibilities should have such a soporific effect on my designated assailant and assassin. I was for that imbecile simply an irrelevance, and not worth bothering about.

Immediately after that split-second, I rejoined the real world, and grappled wildly for the door handle – and found only the way to open the window. I half-heartedly called out things like 'Hey!' or, in French, 'Oi!', but my companion's behaviour since he had swerved off the main road had so scared me, that I did not dare to shake him, nor indeed to touch him in any way. I eventually found the appropriate knob to get out of the car, and retrieved my rucksack from the back seat. I banged both car doors quite loudly in the half-hope of arousing my driver, whom at the same time, with the other half of my mind, I was rather hoping *not* to disturb – on the basis of the proverbial wisdom of letting sleeping dogs lie. Anyhow, there was probably no fear of arousing this particular hound. He was on another planet.

I set out to walk back to the main road. To my surprise, it was only about half a mile away. I would have thought that we had travelled miles through the forest once we had left '*la route nationale*'. When somebody is prey to anxiety bordering on panic, time and distance become very relative. This, as I have discovered in later life, can be a major element in what seem comparatively mild forms of interrogation technique, and even torture.

I walked in to Redon and had something to eat. Then, for a change, I got lucky. A pleasant-looking chap whom I had got talking to in the bistro, where I was eating the French version of a sandwich – and who seemed genuinely interested to hear what the students thought they were up to – volunteered that he was leaving for Laval within the hour and that he would be happy to take me with him. This was indeed good news indeed, because I had been apprehensive about how to get around the urban sprawl of Rennes, which I expected to be even worse than Caen. My new friend was an engineer, who was hoping to build a swimming pool in Laval. When Eoin and I were there, we swam in the Mayenne and were happy with that. When my wife and I returned there in 1993, the town had acquired a magnificent swimming-pool complex – comprising of three outdoor pools, and one indoors. On the other hand, the river by then looked highly polluted. I would love to know if those pools are the work of my friendly engineer.

This was the only time that I got to a campsite before Eoin. Predictably, he had quite a lot of hassle getting through Rennes. From there, he had eventually been saved and chauffeured to Laval by a Jehovah's Witness. They had terrific fun trying to convert each other, and got on like a house on fire. The theological joust, I gather, was a scoreless draw, but full of happy moments nonetheless.

The campsite at Laval was beautiful. Its only drawback was that, for the entire male population, they had only two squat toilets. This could have very well been to encourage a rapid turnover. The strategic arrangements of a squat toilet are not conducive to leisurely reading, or to any unnecessary prolongation of one's business. It constitutes major challenges for some people – me, for instance – in the crucial areas of aim and balance.

That evening in the camp bistro, an Englishman, amongst a cohort of compatriots, was inveighing loudly against the supposed barbarism of the squat toilets. He narrated, in ringing tones, that the previous morning, when he had spread-eagled himself in the required position, and was just knitting his brows in concentration on the matter in hand, an immense rat had suddenly leaped up from the hole in the ground, scuttled between his defenceless buttocks, and squeezed itself out below the door of his cubicle. This recital was greeted with well-bred cries of horror and revulsion from the army of occupation. A Frenchman, who was sitting at the counter, ostensibly reading a newspaper, and taking no part in the proceedings, suddenly raised his head and said clearly, and in perfect English: 'Yes, mon ami, but you *do* have to look at it from the rat's point of view, too.'

I learnt subsequently, and to my amazement, that for the two days we stayed in Laval, Eoin had conducted all his major manoeuvres in the ladies' loo, where, it seems, there were adequate seating arrangements – though I don't suppose he was reading the collected works of Thomas Aquinas while he was 'at it'. He was only caught once *in flagrante delicto*, when, with a spontaneous deviousness of which I would have thought him incapable, he played the part of the innocent abroad. He had the satisfaction of over-hearing the madame who had discovered him explaining to a '*commère*' (a crony) that these 'Englishmen' were so ignorant that they did not even know '*un homme*' from '*une femme*'. As the national interests of the Irish Republic were not at stake, Eoin bore this slight as mere vulgar abuse. Anyhow, he was conscious that, as a cleric, he belonged to what the French themselves call '*le troisième sexe*', and probably had a constitutional right to choose his toilet.

On the road again, and heading for the Loire, we decided to avoid Angers – another urban sprawl – and instead to pass south-east, by the very lovely little town of La Flèche. Even though we were travelling separately, we met up by coincidence in the middle of an open-air market. These markets are such friendly, good-humoured places – the vendors appear to be selling not so much to make money, but because they seem to derive genuine pleasure from it, and because they actually *like* you. Fruit, flowers, and vegetables look so well in their natural environment – outdoors – as do the weather-beaten, smiling *paysans* and *paysannes* who produce them.

'Peasant' is not a demeaning title in France. As a philosopher, I would think that how we esteem the good earth, and the people who derive their livelihood from it, says much about how sane or how bogus we are – or have become.

I remember that we each bought three T-shirts for a song in that market. Amazingly, I discovered recently that I still had one of them, forty years later – in quite good condition – for the simple reason that I had grown too fat for it, once I embarked on my middle-aged spread, at about the age of twenty-seven. My grand-daughter requisitioned the shirt eagerly, saying that it was, 'like, cute'. I have no idea what that means.

After La Flèche, when we had just decided that, for the fifty kilometres to Saumur, we would hitch-hike together again, a police van pulled up, and a side-door slid open. We rapidly scanned our consciences to figure out which of the Ten Commandments, the six Precepts of the Church, or the myriad commands of the Napoleonic Code we had violated.

'*Montez.*'

We mounted obediently, and the van sped off. There were two '*flics*' in uniform and two other men in plain clothes, either police or criminals being delivered to the nearest guillotine. Nobody smiled, or said anything. Everyone sat on wooden benches lining the sides of the van. One of the cops minimally twitched one eye, which we took to be a warm invitation to sit down too. We sat down side by side, even though there would have been more room had we sat one on each side of the van. We needed to feel strength in numbers.

'*Cartes d'identité.*'

We produced our passports. Faces softened fractionally. We knew what that meant. At least we were not English!

Imprudently, I said that we were students.

'Merde!' said the talkative officer.

As Eoin said to me afterwards, 'It was a case of "Don't mention the war!"'

Somehow, we got on to the question of rugby. It emerged that one of the officers had played for France. I had never heard of him, but we nearly ruptured ourselves asking for his autograph. Nineteen sixty-eight was the first year ever that France had won a Five Nations Grand Slam. We made a meal of that, and of the brilliant performances of players like Jo Maso, a then-rising star on the French team.

Gradually, our captors assumed cracked faces, which seemed to indicate that they were smiling. They changed their minds about driving us straight to the guillotine. They revealed themselves to be long-lost friends of ours, intent on driving us the whole way to Saumur. First of all, to celebrate our beautiful new-found long-lost friendship, it was incumbent on the whole wagonload to '*Arroser ça*'. We alighted at a charmingly rustic auberge. Our party consisted of, firstly, Eoin and myself, the four from the back of the van, and two more officers in uniform from the front, to whom we had not yet been introduced. The driver, with a flick of the wrist, turned off his radio contact with headquarters, observing with feeling, '*Ça me fait chier*', the verbal form of '*chienlit*', as employed so recently on national radio and TV by General de Gaulle himself.

On entering the watering hole, it was immediately apparent that our companions were no strangers to either the management or the clientele. Everybody seemed intent on shaking hands with everybody else. The French, of course, are huge shakers of the hand – at least where kissing on the cheek is not really on. I had noticed at the university that whenever two of my professors met casually in the corridor, they would chat affably for thirty seconds, during which they would shake hands at least three times. I muttered to Eoin on the way in, 'Jesus, this is going to cost us an arm and a leg.'

During the next hour, no money changed hands. The six *policiers* consumed at least three – some four – *demis* each. Eoin and I made one *demi* each last the full hour, as much from economy as from temperance. I had visions of us having to pay the full bill, and then being obliged to drive the van up the main street of Saumur, with six policemen lying in the back, speechless drunk and singing the 'Marseillaise'. With a certain surreal appropriateness, it was actually composed in Strasbourg.

We need not have worried – not about the money, anyhow. When it came time to pay, it emerged that the police operated a slate at this particular tavern. No cash appeared, except my proffered few crumpled notes, which were smilingly waved away with the remark that one did not accept money from '*des gosses*'. We knew exactly what the speaker meant. The word 'gossoon' is still current in Ireland, to refer to a young boy.

We need not have worried about the driving, either. Our chauffeur was a model of sobriety, a living witness to the rules of the road. He showed so much consideration and courtesy to other users of the road that he probably *was* drunk. We arrived at Saumur in the late afternoon, and were driven straight to the campsite. This made quite an impression. At the sight of the police vehicle, several campers immediately stopped what they were doing and did something else instead.

The *Camping Municipal* at Saumur is ingeniously situated on an island in the middle of the Loire, and, in fact, in the middle of the town too. This has the double advantage of being near and yet far. The site has been developed over the years, and now includes a super swimming pool, a restaurant, a bar, and a shop. Forty years ago it was simpler, but, even then, most attractive by its very situation.

I remember, also, that it had a football field and goal-posts, where groups of boys and young men seemed to play tirelessly from morning to night. We often joined them – no questions asked, instant friendship. Additionally, there was instant and accurate assessment of our strengths and weaknesses in play. Eoin and I were quickly treated as people who knew what they were about, cheerfully welcomed whenever we appeared. It was the most enjoyable kind of football too – just for the pure fun of it – and generous as well; the smaller kids were allowed to shine.

Using Saumur as a base, we began to visit the chateaux – Saumur itself, of course, but also Langeais, and Chinon, which are not too far away, and where we got to easily 'en stop'. Unencumbered by rucksacks, smiling, and doing our world-famous impersonation of 'nice boys', we had no problems getting lifts. There were far fewer cars on the roads in those days. On the other hand, forty years ago, the war was still very much a living memory. Drivers were much more inclined to help their neighbours.

Eoin produced his secret weapon: a miniature green, white, and orange flag, the Irish tricolour, which he waved encouragingly. Not that anyone knew what it actually was. One chap stopped because he thought we were Italians – at least I looked the part. The Indian flag does have the same three colours, horizontally, and the flag of the Ivory Coast used to have them, back to front. I think that the main point of the tricolour was that it was not the Union Jack. So, whatever else, we were not sons of 'Rule Britannia'. Given the complicated history of those two great nations, it was undoubtedly humiliating for the French to have to be rescued from the clutches of the Reich by – amongst others – 'Perfidious Albion'. For four long years of exile in London during the war, General de Gaulle had to eat industrial quantities of humble pie, which gave someone of his sensitive palate acute indigestion. He did something to restore national pride, and to improve his own self-esteem, by giving the British a bad time when it came to joining the European Community. This was ongoing while Eoin and I were hitch-hiking.

I understood the way the French felt, while also feeling sorry for the Brits. At the age of ten, I was saved from drowning by a nice British couple. Quite inadvertently, the last portion of my anatomy that they dredged up from under the water was my head – where, as is usual, the estuary of my breathing apparatus is situated. My parents thanked the nice couple warmly, whilst I stared at them malevolently, as if they had been so stupid on purpose.

CHAPTER SEVEN

I had known from the beginning of our trip that Eoin planned to visit a house of his religious congregation at Orléans. He knew only one person there – a fellow student at Strasbourg – but it was an opportunity for him to say 'Hi', and to get acquainted with more of his extended family of dedicated missionaries. Saumur was at a manageable distance from Orléans, and our original plan had been for us both to drop by on our way to somewhere else. We had thought then that we would be hitting Orléans on our way south. However, getting to Orléans would now require us to travel north-east, because of adjustments already made to our itinerary. Our project now was to see a few more chateaux – Cheonceaux and Chambord, for instance – but then to resume our thrust to the south, to swim in Mediterranean waters. So, Eoin would still be visiting Orléans, but now by way of a parenthesis in our joint itinerary. I was welcome to accompany him. I decided not to go.

This was because, if we had been passing through – and staying the night – fair enough; my presence would have been legitimate. If, on the other hand, Eoin was making a special pilgrimage to visit his *confrères*, I would have felt like a bit of an intruder into what was a sort of family visit. Besides, I was a little afraid that Eoin's holy family might spot what a heathen I was, be shocked, or – even worse – start working on my conversion. The doomsday scenario might just conceivably be that they would succeed so well as to even recruit me as a missionary and a celibate. That way would have spelt disaster, with me constitutionally incapable of keeping my pants on – forever! Eoin used to tell me, laughing, that in his wild days, St Augustine used to pray, 'Lord, make me chaste – but not yet!'

'Them's my sentiments entirely!' I agreed ruefully, mildly pleased that a saint had said *something* that I could identify with.

And, anyhow, I was very content at Saumur, where I looked forward to a lazy day in the pool, an evening chatting up the available talent in the bistro, and who knows what else . . .

Eoin left from Saumur on Monday 21 June, 1968, at half past eight in the morning. I did look at my watch; I don't know why. His leaving me for a few hours was no big deal. I didn't even get up to see him off. He brought me a mug of coffee in the tent. The last I saw of him was his open sandals, inches from my head, as I lay wrapped up in my sleeping bag. I remember thinking that his toe-nails were so clean, so manly, and so thoroughly *good*. Is that as ridiculous as it sounds? Does it make any possible sense? I don't care. That is what I thought precisely at that moment. That is exactly what I still remember forty years later. Odd as it may sound, Eoin's toes were like an epiphany of his soul for me. I am so very grateful for that memory. I suppose a psychiatrist could make a seven-course meal out of that tasty morsel.

I wonder if that was what Mary Magdalene felt when she

washed the feet of Jesus with her tears, covered them in kisses, then dried them with her hair. I'll tell your psychiatrist friend something for free: neither of us – I mean, neither the gospel woman nor I myself – were thinking about sex.

I had a good day, and a more energetic one than I had expected of myself. I think I realised that, with Eoin gone for the day, I should try to keep busy. Lounging around might not be good for my soul. I hired a bicycle in the town for a few hours, and headed for Fontevraud Abbey, a few miles from Saumur. This was a sort of co-ed monastery in the Middle Ages, with monks and nuns living so near and yet – I hope – so far. Interestingly, it was the abbess, and not the abbot, who wore the pants and called the shots. She was usually of royal blood, and probably had a few battalions to call on if the boyos ever started to get cheeky.

Added attractions were Richard the Lion-Hearted, who is buried at the abbey in the magnificent chapel, under one of these 'sleeping-do-not-disturb' effigies, as is that crook, Henry II of England, and his Queen, Eleanor of Aquitaine. I call this particular Henry a crook, because it was he who began the Norman Conquest of Ireland in eleven hundred and something. And how did he do it? He just asked the Pope, and it just so happened that this particular pope, Adrian VI, was an Englishman himself – surprise, surprise! Even in the twelfth century, it was all down to who you knew. It is a consolation to know that the Holy Spirit has never made the same mistake again. Amongst all the ruffians who have been popes before or since, there has never been another Englishman.

On the way back, I visited the mushroom caves, which were suitably dark and dank, and the horse museum, which is a bit of a bore, unless you are a nag-lover.

I delayed doing anything about supper – even my pre-supper beer – in the hope that Eoin would turn up. His intention was to return that same day, and he had not brought any overnight bag. But he did say that there was a slim possibility – if he found the route unexpectedly difficult – that he might stay the night. I waited until a quarter to eleven, then ate something and drank a beer. I didn't go near the bistro that evening – I was not in the mood. We had a small two-man ridge tent, and it seemed incredibly empty that night. I could have swung the proverbial cat in there.

I waited until four o'clock the following afternoon. By then I was tensed up and uneasy, telling myself that I had nothing to be tensed up or uneasy about. I went through Eoin's rucksack to see if I could find an address or, better still, a telephone number for the monastery at Orléans. I got lucky. There was a letter from the head of that house, assuring Eoin that his community would be glad to welcome him and his *jeune ami* whenever our adventures brought us close enough to pay a visit. There was also an invitation to spend the night if we would like to. The letter was signed, Frédéric Crispin. Most importantly, there was a telephone number.

I went down to the campsite *accueil*, where there were telephones. I dialled, and asked for Monsieur l'Abbé Crispin, without being sure if this was his proper title. It was actually he who answered the phone. Immediately I heard his voice I knew that he was '*sympathique*', and would help in whatever way he could. I told my story. There was a pause. Then he told his story. Yes, Eoin had arrived before midday the previous day, and had had lunch with the community. The universal verdict had been that he was, '*un très gentil garçon*'. After lunch, he had spent some time with his Strasbourg companion, who had shown him round the town for about an hour and a half. Then he himself, Père Crispin, had driven him out of town to the best spot for a lift to Blois, Tours, and eventually Saumur. Eoin had been all set to head for home by, at the latest, four o'clock. With any luck, he could have hoped to be back at base by seven PM, and certainly by nightfall.

I repeat what I have said before, that in those days, forty years ago, the war was still very much a living memory. People *did* give other people lifts. And an obviously fine young man, with an open face and a smile to charm the birds off the bushes, would have no difficulty at all. Besides, I knew from experience that Eoin's prowess at *auto-stop* was little short of awesome.

Père Crispin tried to be reassuring but we both knew that the situation was worrying. Even if Eoin had had an accident, he would have asked somebody to contact either myself or Père Crispin – unless . . . I could not bear to think of the 'unless'.

Eventually Père Crispin said, 'Listen, Andrew, I know that you must be very uneasy. But God is good. Keep up your courage. I will check with the police and with the major hospitals along the route. Are you still staying at the campsite in Saumur?'

'Yes.'

'I will contact you there tomorrow morning. Please God, we will have better news by then. Don't lose heart.'

I went back to my tent, sat on Eoin's sleeping-bag, and cried. When seven o'clock came, I forced myself to eat something. I had hardly eaten for the past twenty-four hours and I was ravenous. Still, I had difficulty shovelling down anything. Then I went down to the campsite bistro to get drunk – and maybe get laid. It was a sordid and familiar routine: I got depressed, I got drunk, and I had sex with whoever was on offer – or even just with myself. Then I slept, and hated myself the next morning. It's what they call 'the vicious circle'.

That night I managed one and a half bottles of beer. Any more and I would have vomited. As for sex, I would like to believe that I was reminded of my conversation with Eoin and was ashamed of myself. But the truth was simpler, and scary. In what I'll call my erroneous or my erotic zone, I now felt just about as extinct as a prehistoric volcano. I realised, suddenly, with something approaching panic, that I was slipping rapidly into a major depression. I had been there just once before – in my late teens – and had very nearly offed myself. This evening in the bistro at Saumur I felt like a guy sliding uncontrollably through loose gravel, towards the edge of a precipice. I was very alone, and very frightened.

My eyes were closed – I don't know for how long – when I sensed that somebody had sat down across the table from me. They did not speak, and I didn't immediately open my eyes. Then I did.

She was middle-aged, handsome rather than beautiful, with silvery grey hair tight to her head. It was a good face: strong but feminine, no make-up, with delicate lines around hazel eyes that were wise and compassionate. I don't remember how she was dressed. I do remember wondering what someone like her was doing in a campsite bistro, full of jerks like me, there to get drunk and laid. She asked me: 'What is wrong, Andrew?'

So I told her all about Eoin. Not just about him being lost, but everything, about the fact that we had always been togeth-er as long as I could remember, that we had been to the same schools, played on the same teams, knocked around with the same gang. I even heard myself saying, 'I always took him for granted, like a brother. It's only in the last ten days or so that I've realised just how much he means to me.'

'Do you love him?' she asked gently.

'Yes, I do.'

My unhesitating answer amazed me. I had never dared to say that I loved Eoin. Not to him. Not even to myself. Here I was telling it to this total stranger.

'Is it sexual?' she asked. Immediately, I was certain that the question did not come from a vulgar interest. I even had a feeling that she knew the answer to her question already, and that she really wanted to help me to see into my own heart.

I said, 'I've never thought about Eoin that way. I'm just – not like that – if you know what I mean.'

'Is he?' she persisted.

'I don't know,' I answered. 'I don't think so. What I *do* know is that this has been the purest love that I have ever known, and I've had some pretty impure ones. I know what I'm talking about.'

Time passed. My eyes were closed again. The woman was holding my two hands clasped on the table between us. She was speaking. She said that Eoin and I had been uniquely privileged to share such a friendship, and that she was sure that it had been very important for him. I noticed that she spoke in the past tense, as if Eoin were . . . and yet we both knew that he was alive. She said that I would have to let Eoin go, and that this was how he would have wished it. She also said that Eoin's love would always be precious to me, for as long as I lived. And so indeed it has been.

The woman spoke for a long time, gently, and was silent, too. I cannot remember many specific things that she said. What I do know is that her words, at the same time, brought me sorrow and healing, pain and peace, in the depths of my heart.

There was silence.

When I opened my eyes she was gone. I am almost certain I never told her that my name was Andrew. I finished my beer, and it did me good. I went back to my tent, and slept soundly.

I woke at about half past six in the morning. The birds were doing their dawn-chorus routine. It was cool and fresh in the tent. A light breeze was tickling the poplar trees. They hummed in soft alto. I lay on my back, and wondered at how I had so over-reacted the previous evening, wanting to get drunk, then laid, then nearly staging a major depression, and somehow accepting that Eoin was certainly dead. I would never accept that Eoin was dead – never!

And who was that woman? Where did she come from? How did she know the right questions to ask me? And why was I so ready to talk to her about Eoin and about our friendship, with such complete honesty that I had learned things about myself that I had not even realised until then? I believed that she was surely an angel sent by Eoin – when he saw how badly I was coping with my grief. It was certainly a grace, as we Catholics would call it: a radical breakthrough to wisdom and wholeness.

So Eoin was still alive, OK? I sprang out of my sleeping bag and went for a shower. No more negative, craven thinking, I promised myself.

Shortly after ten o'clock, I was coming out of the campsite reception, where I had been explaining about Eoin and saying that I was expecting an important telephone call. The girl in charge was very sweet. She tried to reassure me that all would end well, and she promised that they would hail me on the PA the minute the call came through.

I was turning away from *l'accueil*, when I saw a young ascetic-looking man, prematurely grey, trotting up the steps to the reception. It was a mutual case of 'Dr Livingstone, I presume.' By some chemistry, we recognised each other at the same moment. It was Père Frédéric Crispin. He had driven over from Orléans. Having checked quickly that neither of us had any good or bad news – or indeed any firm news at all – we went to sit in the bistro for a cup of coffee, and a discussion about what we were going to do now.

Immediately, Père Crispin said that I was to call him Fred. He reported that, through the police, he had checked every hospital, clinic, or morgue to which Eoin could have been brought, if he had been injured or killed on the road from Orléans to Saumur. All results were negative. Another possibility was a hit-and-run, where the driver – after he had hit and before he had run – had hidden the body in the undergrowth at the side of the road.

'Very unlikely,' Fred commented, 'on a busy road with cars passing constantly.'

'So, what else?' I asked. 'Could he have been kidnapped?'

'For what? Fred asked. 'Kidnapping is an extremely troublesome crime. It is only worth somebody's sweat if it's going to yield a lot of money. Is Eoin's family rich?'

'No,' I said. 'His dad is something in the Department of Finance. They're comfortably off, but nothing special.'

The priest seemed to hesitate. Then he said, 'Eoin is a good-looking boy. The police say – and it is only a long shot but it has been known to happen – he just may have been sexually molested and killed.'

He added with obvious reluctance, 'When I described Eoin for them, they said that good-looking blonde boys are "collectors' items for some perverts in a nation of brunettes." I am quoting the actual words used to me.'

'Jesus Christ!' I cried in anguish. Before I could help it, I added, 'I've heard fucking everything now!'

This last bit was in English. Luckily, I don't think that Fred understood it. The French were hopeless at languages until the European thing really caught on – which was not until a few years later.

The priest concluded: 'The only other thing is, if Eoin went into the bushes at the side of the road to have a pee, and had an accident, fell down a hole, broke his leg, was bitten by a snake, was attacked by a wild boar, or even had one of these freak cardiac-arrest things... You sometimes hear of that with young fellows, seemingly as healthy as could be, who still drop dead suddenly during football matches.'

'Perhaps we should be out beating the bushes, searching,' I suggested.

Fred replied, 'That is difficult to organise. It needs a lot of people. For a child, perhaps, or for somebody known and loved in a locality, yes, maybe. For a foreign hitch-hiker, an adult?' The priest raised his shoulders in a typically French gesture of doubt amounting to scepticism.

When Fred asked me if I intended to continue my tour of France without Eoin, I felt tears stinging at my eyes. I dropped my head and said, 'No.'

'Well then, Andrew, come back with me to Orléans. We shall leave all kinds of messages with the police and at the campsite to alert us if there is any news. Meanwhile, I will telephone to St Augustine's – our house of studies in Dublin – where, naturally, Eoin's family will be well known. I will ask the Father Superior, Willie Kelly, to call out in person to Eoin's parents and to break the news gently, being as hopeful as we can honestly be – which, I am afraid, is not very. He is an excellent man, whom I have known for years. You can call his parents later, and your own family as well. Stay for a few days at Orléans, and we'll see what we can organise in the line of a search-party.

I cried again when I was packing up Eoin's clothes and his few possessions. How little he had, and how anybody in the world could want to harm such an inoffensive, defenceless, and unselfish person. And how little we all have to pit against the cruelty and evil of the world!

CHAPTER EIGHT

Fred's community at Orléans were fine people. There were seven or eight of them, and they treated me like next-of-kin. Even though Eoin had only stayed a few hours with them, they each had something nice to say about him, which I stored up carefully to tell his parents.

Meanwhile, Fred himself was not letting the grass grow under his feet. He had a friend of a friend who was a big shot in the army, or in the Ministry of Defence. This chap promised that within twenty-four hours he could get twenty or thirty rookies doing their national service, out and scouring the hedgerows from Orléans to Saumur.

Overnight, there was another encouraging development, when the police located a driver who had picked up a hitch-hiker on the Monday afternoon, on the outskirts of Orléans, heading for Saumur. This was almost certainly Eoin. Everything fitted: age, physical appearance, character, and personality. This man had driven Eoin as far as the other side of Blois, and they had arrived there by five o'clock in the afternoon. This reduced – by at least a third – the territory to be covered by the searchers, as well as further sharpening the time parameters for the day when Eoin went missing.

As promised, the search began the following day. There were twenty-three rookies, delighted to be doing something different from their monotonous daily grind, which seemed to consist of executing never-ending press-ups at the behest of some scream-ing sadist, mopping out latrines for the honour and greater security of the French Republic, or just being bored out of their tree. The party was subdivided into four subgroups responsible for different segments of the terrain to be covered. Fred had arranged a car, so that Eoin's friend from Strasbourg, two other volunteers from the Orléans community, and I myself could join in the search.

Considering the fact that Eoin was making for Saumur, and traffic going that way was moving along the north side of the road, the young officer in charge of the operation concentrated his main troops in the thickets bordering the flow of traffic on that side, towards the west. He also detailed one member in each of the four search parties to pass more rapidly along the (south) side of the road, just in case Eoin had strayed from the more likely itinerary. We did nine hours that first day, broken by a suprisingly appetising lunch, dropped from a military vehicle to each of the groups wherever they had reached that morning.

I liked the attitude of the young French soldiers. They were extremely thorough in their search, surprisingly respectful of the fact that Eoin was a trainee man of God, and sensitive in their treatment of the chap from Strasbourg and myself once they heard that we had both known Eoin as a friend. They seemed also to be generous between themselves, cheerful, and trying to make the ordeal of compulsory military service more bearable for those less suited to the sheer mindlessness of it.

The Orléans party were tired after their nine-hour stint. We had showers, and went out to eat in a little restaurant where my companions were clearly no strangers. During the meal several people came up to ask how the search was going, and I could see them telling other customers what was happening as they returned to their places. A ripple of concern and solidarity seemed to spread through the restaurant, and by the end of the evening, I had pretty well told everyone mine and Eoin's life story. Wasn't it the same story after all? The *patron* of the restaurant refused any payment for our meal. When I tried to thank him, he simply said, '*Tu as de la peine, petit gars*', and embraced me.

It was after lunch on the second day of our search, and our group was approaching Vouvray and Tours, which marked the boundary of our sector. An army jeep pulled up; it was the young officer in command of the search. He spoke to me very gently. 'We have found what seems to be a shallow grave, very recently dug. I fear that it may hold your friend.'

'A grave?' I stammered, and continued, inanely, 'Who would bury him . . . and why?'

The officer put a hand on my arm.

'Come. There will be time for all those questions afterwards. Now we must see if it is your friend, and bring him amongst family and friends, and make him more comfortable, so to speak. Yes?'

'Yes,' I said, and followed him.

Eoin's Strasbourg friend had been standing near me during this exchange. He did not offer to accompany me. I felt sorry for him, and I certainly make no judgement of anyone's motives in such an agonising situation. Perhaps he just could not face seeing the dead body. Or perhaps, on the other hand, he felt that it was my call whether he should come with me or not. Maybe I should have asked him to come, and maybe he was hurt that I did not . . . I don't even remember the guy's name. I wonder whether that is particularly significant – have I just edited him out of Eoin's life? Out of his death? Was I even jealous of his friendship for Eoin? Is that why I didn't ask him to come with me? I don't know the answers to any of these questions. When tragedy strikes, we are exposed, in all our ambiguous and ambivalent colours, and we recognise in ourselves things that we would probably be more comfortable not to have known.

The officer, whose name was Joe, could not have been much older than Eoin and myself, perhaps in his late twenties. In the jeep he told me that the grave had been discovered near Bourgueil, a little place scarcely further from Saumur than Fontevraud, where I had cycled on Monday.

Joe said: 'He nearly made it.'

I felt sick.

Then Joe said, as compassionately as he could: 'Andrew, they had not uncovered the body when I was leaving to collect you. I must warn you that it may not be a pretty sight. We don't know what injuries Eoin may have suffered . . . or what may have been done to him. Also, remember that Eoin has probably been dead for five days. In this hot weather you know, even though he has been covered . . . '

He left that sentence unfinished. I was touched that this soldier, who could just as easily have said nothing at all, had the thoughtfulness to try to prepare me for what could be quite a shock. Even in the middle of receiving such a grim warning, I could not help smiling at the Frenchman's heroic and incredibly inaccurate rendering of my friend's name. He gave it four syllables – one for each letter. He continued, 'I am saying this to help you. Try to say in your mind – these things are what my friend has suffered, and they are ugly. But I will give him victory over this evil, by remembering him the way he was when last we laughed together.'

I asked Joe, 'Were you in Algeria?

'Yes, I was,' he answered, 'at the most atrocious time. I saw things that nobody should ever have to see. So that is why I am talking to you this way.'

Eoin had been buried hastily, in a grave eighteen inches under, so, perhaps three feet deep. The grave had been dug with a sharp spade. If it had been left until the end of the summer, it would probably never have been found. By the time I arrived, Eoin had been taken out of the hole, and was now lying on his back at some distance away from it. This was at the request of the police, who had been summoned once the grave had been found, and who did not want the surface area in the vicinity of the grave to be 'contaminated' – whatever that might mean.

Eoin was fully clothed in what I had last seen him wearing. He was not ashen white, as I had expected, but a dirty grey tint. His eyes were half-closed, and his mouth half-open. His face, expressionless, did not betray either suffering or the joys of heaven already begun. There was no visible injury to his head or face, though I could see some clay in his mouth, nostrils, ears and eyes. I heard later that some of the young soldiers had wanted to clean his face, at least, but were instructed not to, lest they destroy any evidence.

When I approached, this discussion was obviously concluding.

'What kind of evidence?' one rookie asked skeptically.

The detective Inspector sighed, then gave it to him straight.

'For instance, traces of somebody else's skin, blood, spittle, pubic hair, urine, excrement, or semen on the boy's face, or in his mouth.'

The young soldier's own mouth fell open. He did a double-take, and then got sick, no doubt contaminating the scene.

Every time I hear the Gospel account of the raising of Lazarus, I think of Eoin – not that anyone raised him from the dead – but because of Martha's comment that it was already the fourth day, and 'He will stink'. In Eoin's case, it was the fifth day, and, yes, there was a sort of vague too-sweet smell. It was not very noticeable in the open air. In a confined space, like a bedroom or even a chapel, it could be quite distressing. I knew, too, that it would get worse before it got better.

'Don't worry,' Joe whispered, '*le croque-mort*' will fix that.' That is what the French call an undertaker: a "stiff-muncher". I understood, then, that I would probably be the last member of Eoin's wider "family" to see him on this earth. By the time he could be repatriated, he would be "too far gone". Besides, I remembered hearing that when corpses are flown home, it has to be done in a sealed lead coffin, which is not usually opened again.

I knelt down quickly and kissed Eoin on the forehead. I did this for myself but, even more so, I did it for his mother and his dad. He was the light of their eyes. I would have liked to kiss him on the lips – and I certainly felt no repugnance to do that – smell or no smell, contamination or no contamination. But the angle was wrong. I suppose, to be truthful, I had some fear of what all those men might think: there were about seventeen of them standing around, between members of the search party and the police.

I underestimated them. When I had solemnly identified Eoin to the satisfaction of the police, nearly every French person there came up to me and expressed his sympathy. Some shook my hand, some patted me on the back or on the shoulder, some hugged me, and some kissed me on both cheeks. I tried to thank them. I know that Eoin's parents later wrote a beautiful letter to Joe, the young officer, and asked him to circulate it to all the searchers, which he did.

That evening I called Eoin's parents from Orléans. They had already accepted that he was most probably dead, and it came as a relief to them that at least he had been found, and that there was no mark of violence on his body. I suppose I told a white lie there, because I had only seen his face, and, after all, you cannot kill somebody without exercising violence on some part of his body. We talked for a long time. Both Eoin's father and his mother said repeatedly, and in many different ways, that they were so happy that he and I had spent those last few weeks together.

'You were almost brothers,' they told me again and again.

'We used to call you Tweedledum and Tweedledee,' Eoin's Mum said.

'Or, other times, the Terrible Twins,' his Dad tried to laugh.

When I plucked up my courage and told Eoin's Mum that, earlier that day, I had kissed Eoin goodbye and Godspeed for her and for his Dad, there was a long silence, so much so that I began to panic. I thought, with sudden fright, that in spite of my good intentions, they would surely resent what I had done as an unbearable presumption, a usurpation. 'How could I have got it so wrong?' I wondered, aghast.

When Eoin's Mum spoke again, she was very composed. She said, 'Andrew, I think that this is the most beautiful thing that you could ever do for us. May God bless you always, sweetheart.'

She hung up, and I called my own mother, and cried for twenty minutes into her ear.

CHAPTER NINE

The next day I had a long interview with the police, which they eventually froze into a formal statement that I had to sign. Factually, I suppose, it was accurate enough, but it wasn't me, and it certainly wasn't Eoin. To read it, you would think that he was just any old Tom, Dick or Harry. I suppose that is why they call death 'the leveller'. Dying is the most democratic thing that you can do. Everyone manages it sooner or later. I fought against the thought that, in dying, Eoin had ceased to be unique, and had become just another item on a conveyor belt, a suitcase at the airport, or even less – a mere statistic.

There was worse to come. The following day another *flic* came around. He began to bully me with suggestions that Eoin and I were just a pair of 'little friends' who'd had a lovers' quarrel. According to this *poulet* (another, even less complimentary term for a policeman), I was the only person within hundreds of miles who knew Eoin and could have had the slightest motive for killing him. I shouted at this cretin that you did not need to have been introduced to a person to have a reason for killing him.

'What other possible reason could there be?' he persisted. 'A hitch-hiker who doesn't even have enough money for a bus or a train! Why would anyone kill him?'

I replied with a string of obscenities, which – fortunately, I thought – my tormentor did not understand. In French, I said, 'I don't know what reason Eoin was killed for. It makes no sense for me at all. And that is precisely what you are paid for – to fucking find out!'

I know I was in a rage. It was a rude awakening from being treated with sensitivity, and embraced as Eoin's close friend, and, practically, next of kin. Yes, there was an element of hurt pride in my reaction. Still, to be treated as Eoin's murderer was totally unexpected. It shocked and upset me more than I can say.

He did not go away.

'I would advise you to calm yourself, Monsieur. You are in serious trouble. Is it true that when the victim's body was found, you kissed his face?'

I know that my mouth fell open from sheer disbelief.

'Jesus,' I said in English, continuing in French, 'just how low are you prepared to stoop?'

'Answer the question, please.'

'Yes, I did kiss him. What does that convey to your filthy mind?'

He answered immediately, slamming a further question over the net to me. 'It conveys a very special relationship, when you kiss a corpse four or five days dead. What was the nature of that relationship? Were you perhaps apologising for having lost your temper and murdering him?'

A phrase of the Gospel came to me: 'Cast not your pearls before swine.' There was no way that I could communicate to this swine the sort of relationship that I had had with Eoin – all of our lives – and what I was trying to do for his grieving parents, for Eoin's sake.

I simply said, in English, 'Mind your own fucking business, will you?'

To my surprise, he seemed satisfied, and turned to another topic.

'You hired a bicycle and cycled to Fontevraud, yes?'

'Yes. Is that a crime?'

'Have you ever hired a bicycle in your life before?'

'What kind of a question is that?'

'Answer, please.'

'I don't know – probably not.'

'Had you arranged to meet Eoin at Fontevraud?'

'Of course not.'

'But you admit that you were in Fontevraud that day?'

'Listen! I don't *admit* it. I'd bloody well *say* it to anyone who wants to hear it. Yes, I was in Fontevraud that day. What's the big bloody deal?

'You do realise that the place where your friend was killed and buried on that very day is just a few miles from Fontevraud? Such a coincidence!'

'What kind of an imbecile are you? Are you seriously suggesting that I met Eoin at Fontevraud, where he had broken his journey – hitch-hiking all the way from Orléans – to engage in a little supplementary culture? I suppose, the way you figure it, he must have been hoping that when we had finished seeing the sights, I would prop him up on the cross-bar of my specially hired bicycle, and ferry him the whole way back to Saumur.'

He tried to interrupt me – but I was not going to be stopped. I shouted him down.

'*Instead of which*, according to your crazy logic, I murdered him – we don't even know yet how, until we get the result of the autopsy – and then for some idiotic reason, I carried his dead body several miles on my fucking bicycle, in the wrong direction, and buried him at Bourgueil, with a shovel that just happened to drop from heaven. If you believe all that crap, you'd believe anything. *plus*, I was back at the campsite and had given back my bicycle, *hours* before Eoin ever reached . . . wherever he did reach.'

'Ah, how do you know that?' he challenged.

'I know it – and you know it perfectly well too – because Père Crispin told me that the guy who gave Eoin a ride as far as Blois arrived there at five o'clock PM By that time I was back in Saumur, playing football with at least a dozen other people who will remember me. So, will you give me a break, and stop this bullshit?'

I saw a flicker of a smile on the policeman's face. He did not say anything else but – to my astonishment – he pressed my arm in a friendly way as he made for the door.

Later in life, I was to learn more about interrogation techniques, including the effectiveness of alternating between Mister Nice Guy and Mister Nasty Bastard. Mr Nasty Bastard was only doing his job, I suppose, though he was so good at it that I bet he enjoyed it. Mister Nice Guy confided to me months afterwards that it took only five minutes to convince Mister Nasty Bastard that I was telling the truth, that he liked me, and that he admired my 'Irish spirit'. I'm never quite sure what people mean when they say that. Mister Nice Guy also told me that Mister Nasty Bastard trained in New York for three years, spoke perfect English, and fully understood all the foul names I was calling him in that language. Perhaps that is what he meant by 'Irish spirit'. I'm not sure if I should be pleased or proud about that.

I stayed around in Orléans for another two or three days, enough to know when Eoin's body would be released, and when and where the funeral would be taking place. Fortunately, Eoin's religious congregation, specialising, as they do, in missionary activities in far-away places, have insurance policies covering the costs for repatriation of what we call, grotesquely, 'the remains' of worn-out padres – even murdered ones – from almost anywhere in the world. The costs are, apparently, horrendous. They do indeed include a sealed lead coffin – as I had heard – which must weigh a ton and cost a fortune.

The funeral service would be held in the chapel of Eoin's religious community in Dublin, which had been a dance hall in the nineteen fifties, but had been very successfully reinvented as a place of worship. It had the essential requirement of being sufficiently spacious to hold the very large crowd that was expected, and did indeed materialise, on the day.

At the request of Eoin's family, he would not be buried with his fellow missionaries, but in a plot that his parents now bought in Deansgrange Cemetery, intending that they themselves would eventually be reunited with him. It had space, too, for his married sister, if she had seen enough of her husband by the time she came to die.

The day before I left Orléans, Mister Nice Guy, whose real name was Inspector Michel Péron, called to see Fred and myself, to fill us in on how the investigation was going. The cause of death, he said, was a broken neck. Death would have been instantaneous, as in hanging.

'This injury was almost certainly inflicted deliberately, and by someone who knew exactly what he was doing. A blow, a kick, or a violent jerk is all that was needed.'

'What about a whiplash thing?' I asked. 'If you have a violent collision – and especially if you are wearing one of these new-fangled seat-belts – I'm told that you can suffer a whiplash that can break your neck.'

'Well,' the Inspector answered mildly, 'I am not a medical expert, but the doctor who performed the autopsy absolutely excluded any such explanation. Besides, there is no evidence that any car in the vicinity had been involved in a violent collision, and there was literally no other injury on the body, which there surely would have been in the event of a collision – whether a seat-belt was worn or not.'

Fred, who had so far kept silence, intervened. 'Andrew, I think we can exclude accident. If there is an accidental death, you ring for the ambulance. You do not bury the victim in the middle of the night in an unmarked grave.'

The Inspector nodded his assent.

'I suppose you're right,' I agreed. 'The only thing that matters, then, is who murdered Eoin, and why? I cannot think of anyone – no matter how deranged – wanting to murder him. You could not want to murder him, even if you tried.'

'We are not there yet,' the Inspector answered, 'but I can tell you one thing. He was a nice-looking young man, but it wasn't for sex. There are no signs of a struggle, and no trace of, *euh*, the customary marks of such an, *euh*, attack.'

The Inspector had become noticeably coy about 'the customary marks of such an attack', but he glanced at me as he said it, and I felt fairly sure that he was acquitting me of having sodomised Eoin, at least any time recently. Mister Nasty Bastard had been quite explicit about the possibility that Eoin and I had been lovers, and that I had murdered him, maybe because he had run after another boy or – *quelle horreur* – a girl! Love, whether heterosexual or homosexual, is always a fertile source of motives for murder.

I knew that a lot of people – even forty years ago – would have shrugged their shoulders and said, 'Well, so what?' But I did care about this insinuation. I did not really understand Eoin's commitment to celibacy, but I was certain that – for him at least – it was right. It was his way to both give and receive love. Eoin was utterly sincere, and profoundly serious about what he believed to be his vocation.

Inspector Péron had some interesting things to report about the whodunit aspect of the investigation.

'People do not normally travel with spades and shovels in the boot of their cars, on the off-chance that they will meet someone whom they badly want to murder and bury. Assuming that Eoin was killed on the evening of the Monday, the murderer might have had trouble procuring an implement late in the day to dig his grave, without arousing suspicion. No local farmer has any recollection of being asked to lend a spade, or is missing one from his farmyard. On the other hand, the murderer might have had a different problem: that of concealing the body until he could get a spade and bury it. One possibility is that the body spent the night in the boot of the murderer's car.'

Fred asked a question. 'Why did the assassin bury the body?'

The Inspector continued in the same level tones. 'Surely, that is obvious. Without a body, we cannot be sure of what became of our young friend. With a body, we can make considerable headway in knowing what has happened. We can begin to piece together a certain profile of the killer. Death, as a result of one clean blow. Who could achieve that?'

Without waiting for an answer to his question, the Inspector continued. 'If the burial was done immediately, that means that the murderer had access to an implement, and that suggests that he was a local person. If, on the other hand, he had to wait until the morning, that means that he either travelled to where he could find a spade, or bought one without arousing suspicion. If, in the interval, the killer concealed the body in the boot of his car, that must be a reasonably big car.

'And now, let us introduce another factor that contrives to make these assumptions somewhat more plausible. We made particular note that the grave was dug with a sharp spade. The edges are very clean and strong. A new spade, perhaps? Ah yes, if we assume that this person was not from this area, perhaps his only way to acquire a spade – without talking to a local farmer and arousing suspicions – was to buy it somewhere. So, where would he have bought it? Not in the nearest little huckster's shop – that would certainly be remembered. No, he would have gone to the nearest big store, where there would be a good chance of remaining anonymous and unremarked. We could try Tours. In fact, we first tried Saumur. It is nearer and simpler. *Et alors, voilà!*'

I cannot remember the store that the Inspector named. It may have been Rallaye, but I am not sure that the Rallaye chain even existed in France so long ago. The point is that it was one of the bigger stores, where a purchaser could have a better chance of not being remembered.

The policeman continued in the same methodical manner. 'The fact is that on the Tuesday, the day after this young man failed to reach the campsite in Saumur, a spade of exactly the width and curve of the implement with which his grave was dug, was bought in Saumur. Admittedly, there is nothing unusual about the tool – except perhaps that it was new and sharp. The only reason that the young shop assistant noticed and remembered this particular purchase was that the buyer arrived immediately after the shop opened, at eight o'clock in the morning. It seems that the gardening department almost never does business until mid-morning or later. Perhaps this was the first mistake that the perpetrator of this crime made: to be too eager to bury his victim, and to get out of the Loire Valley as fast as he could. And he made a second mistake.'

'What was that?' Fred asked, the ghost of a smile playing on his lips, both sceptical and impressed by the ingenuity of the policeman's reconstructions. They were both very typical Frenchmen.

'No small talk,' the Inspector answered. 'Gardeners like to tell you all about it. This chap sang dumb so as not to be noticed, so he was!

We both burst out laughing at the sheer cleverness of the argument.

I asked the Inspector, 'Do you have a description of this man?'

'Of course. Two metres tall, powerfully built – he would need a large car – greying fair hair, mid-to-late fifties, vigorous, unsmiling.'

'Not a bundle of laughs,' I commented redundantly.

'I can tell you one more thing. The place where your young friend was killed, or more accurately, where he was buried – we are not sure where he was killed – is an expanse of about three hundred metres long, and a hundred metres wide, of dense veg-etation. It was probably originally designed as a wind-break, but the trees have mostly been cut down, and now it is more of an impenetrable thicket than anything else. You were a member of the search party, so you will probably have noticed that there is a narrow lane just before this maquis begins, to give access from the road to the field that lies behind it. A local farmer has told us that there was a big black car – a Citroën, he thinks – parked in that laneway for an hour or more on that Tuesday morning. He does not know when it was eventually driven away, nor did he see the driver.

The fact that the car was there for such a long period was strange. Sometimes cars do drive into this lane, so that the occupants can get out and relieve themselves. Occasionally, people make it a site for a picnic or for romantic moments. You will note that the grave is about twenty metres from the lane, but that even two or three metres in from the laneway, one is hidden. It would be the work of a few minutes for somebody strong enough to haul the body from the boot of the car, and to get it under cover. There are no traces of a body being dragged from the laneway to the site of the grave. I would guess that a big powerful man could carry that body, perhaps over his shoulder, for that distance. The boy had a light frame. We have weighed him, of course – sixty-four kilos, or about ten stone – as you would say it. A fireman could do that, and even walk down a ladder at the same time.'

The priest nodded his head slowly, seeming to agree, but decided to play the devil's advocate.

'If, as you surmise, the driver of this black car was not from this locality, how did he choose such an ideal place to bury the body? The site was hidden from view, and, within a few weeks, the vegetation would have closed over it again and it would have been very difficult to find – even for our searchers.'

It was the Inspector's turn to nod his head, indicating that he accepted the challenge and was willing and able to answer it.

'I think, Mon Père, that this is the wrong question. Initially, this driver is not looking for a good place to bury his victim: he is looking for a secluded place to murder him. You cannot murder someone on the side of a busy road without attracting unfavourable attention. If we assume that – for whatever reason – this driver has decided to kill that young man, he will be looking for somewhere to park his car out of the public gaze while he does so. He sees this lane to his right. He turns into it. His passenger is, no doubt, unaware of his intentions. He thinks that they have stopped to urinate. In fact, the boy's fly buttons were open when he was found, and there was urine on his leg and down his trousers. He was taken from behind and died instantly, relieving himself. I would describe that as a happy death, indeed, strangely symbolic.'

'Symbolic of what?' I inquired. But the Inspector did not answer. He continued with his train of thought.

'It was then, I think, that the murderer decided that – two for the price of one – this would be a good place not only for murdering his victim but for disposing of his body as well. He has no spade, so he would have to return the next day. Whether he carried the body into the thicket immediately, or whether he stowed it in his car overnight, we do not know. I think the latter is more likely.'

Inspector Péron accepted a glass of calvados after his analytical exertions. The priest, meanwhile, summarised the exposé which the policeman had just delivered.

'So, a killing on Monday evening, the purchase of a new spade early on Tuesday morning by a powerful man in his mid-fifties, probably not from this area. On the same Tuesday morning, there is a big black car, a Citroën, parked in the vicinity of the grave, which has been dug with an implement identical – or very similar – to the new spade.

'Each of these factors may be completely independent of the others, but there is an undoubted convergence, real or coincidental.'

As a budding philosopher myself, I admired the logic and the sheer analytical skills of both men. The downside of this is that, once the French have decided that you are logically guilty, it is very difficult to reverse that decision. Once the French police arrest somebody on suspicion of murder, he is routinely called '*l'assassin*' in all the newspapers.

I asked the tough question.

'But what about the motive: why would anyone want to murder a harmless hitch-hiker, and why on earth would somebody want to kill Eoin? He was the friendliest and most loveable person in the world.'

The Inspector did his shrug-and-uplifted-hands routine.

'It is baffling, I agree. If it was for robbery or for sex, we could understand it, but we are left with very unlikely explanations. A case of mistaken identity, or some other sort of tragic mistake, a deranged person, a fanatic of some hue or colour, or an old-fashioned sadist. Except sadists do not kill instantaneously: they like to enjoy at their leisure. It is the secret burial – so efficiently executed, though clearly not anticipated – that makes nonsense of most of these explanations. We shall have to see.'

CHAPTER TEN

I don't want to drag out the agony about Eoin's funeral, and how we mourned him. He was only twenty-three but it was extraordinary to see the great multitude of people whose lives he had touched deeply – not just because he was murdered – but simply by being such a terrific guy. I often wonder what God thinks he is doing. John Paul – not the Pope, for once – the philosopher, John-Paul Sartre, says that *'le monde est mal fait'*, meaning that the world is badly made. I tend to agree. Certainly, if God was a defender with Manchester United, he would be sacked out of hand: too many own goals! For me, and for many people, what happened to Eoin was one of God's more scandalous own goals. A *'scandalum'* is, literally, something put in your way, that you trip over. Who told me that? Eoin, when it didn't seem to matter tuppence.

Of course, I travelled back for the funeral. I stayed nearly three months in Ireland. Strasbourg had nothing happening academically, and the pain of Eoin's death was still so fresh for me. I needed family.

It was mid-summer in that year, 1968, before I thought of Eoin's camera. I had already developed whatever photographs I had taken of our camping trip, and shared them with Eoin's parents. There were some excellent shots of Eoin. He was very photogenic, because he was always engaging with whoever was photographing him, and usually smiling. But what about his own camera? I had quite forgotten it, perhaps because, presumably, there would be no photographs of himself on the film. I knew that he had that camera on more or less permanent loan from one of his senior confrères, who had become a chronic invalid. It was quite a good camera, and he was at least a competent photographer in the days when you had to be. On the road, Eoin usually carried that camera in its pouch at his waist, looped to his belt.

Eoin had not taken even a small bag when he was setting out for Orléans. As an expert hitch-hiker, he fully expected to return the same day. He had said – jokingly, I hope – 'If I don't get back, surely somebody will share a toothbrush with me.' He just had the clothes he'd stood up in, and distributed between various pockets, his passport, some money, a rosary beads, a comb, sunglasses, a tube of sun-screen, and a handkerchief. At least, that's all the police found when the grave was opened. These items were returned to me in a paper bag, as 'next-of-kin'. Grotesquely, this happened on the very same day as Mister Nasty Bastard was accusing me of having murdered their owner.

I cannot swear that Eoin was wearing that camera at his belt when he took to the road, because I didn't notice, one way or the other. Still, I am sure that he was wearing it because, when that awful thing happened, and when I was packing Eoin's bits and pieces into his rucksack and rolling up the tent, I did not find the camera.

Two months later, when the question of the camera eventually crossed my mind, I rang Father Fred in Orléans. He said that Eoin had not left the camera there, but also said that he distinctly remembered Eoin wearing a pouch at his belt, and wondered what it was.

About a week later, I was surprised to receive a call at home in Dublin from Inspector Péron. I didn't know how he had gotten my telephone number, or maybe I gave it to him myself – I had to fill up enough forms while making my statement to the police. The Inspector told me that Fred had reported to him what I had said about Eoin's camera. This had struck a chord, and he had returned to the notes that he had made at the time when Eoin's body was found. Those notes confirmed that, not only were Eoin's fly buttons open – as we know he was in the act of urinating when he was killed – but his belt was also open and undone, from the first two loops on his trouser waistband.

The Inspector continued: 'You don't open your belt when you just want to do pee-pee. At first, we thought that this young man had possibly been interfered with – sexually. On further examination of the body and the clothes, we excluded that supposition – rightly, I think. But the fact that the belt was unbuckled did still continue to puzzle us. We realise now that this missing camera was, in fact, also the missing link; it supplies a comprehensive explanation of all the facts.

'The only possible conclusion is that the opening of the fly buttons, in order to urinate, came first: the opening of the belt and its detachment from the loops on the trouser waistband came later, when the boy was already dead. This can only mean that, after Eoin was dead, the killer took his camera. Why? Was this a very valuable camera? I hardly think so – given the general lifestyle of the young man. Or, had some photograph been taken with that camera which the killer would find compromising, even incriminating? In other words, was this boy killed for his camera? That is precisely the question.'

I could only say: 'That sounds both incredible and yet likely.'

Later that day, I called to see Father Declan O'Keeffe, the missionary who had lent or, in fact, given his camera to Eoin. I had met him briefly at the funeral and had immediately taken to him. He was one of these men who, no matter how old they get, retain their interest in life, their optimism, and their belief in young people. I could well imagine him and Eoin getting on very well together. They were birds of a feather: cheerful, always prepared to take people at their best, and completely devoid of resentment or envy. Several people confirmed to me later that the old man was Eoin's chief role-model in the congregation.

The first time that I really talked to the Padre was on that day in mid-summer, when I had eventually remembered about Eoin's camera. The police had reached the conclusion that, for some mysterious reason, he had been murdered because of it. I wanted to know from Father O'Keeffe if the camera was particularly valuable – even to the point of making it worth somebody's while to kill for it.

'Well,' he chuckled, 'you would need to be pretty hard up to murder for that camera. I cannot imagine a grey-haired executive in a big Citroën killing for it. I bought it in Hong Kong around 1950 – it was quite old by the time I gave it to Eoin, but still good. He sent us a few photos as soon as he got to Strasbourg, to show us where he was "hanging out", as you guys say nowadays. They were fine.

'I paid ten for that camera – dollars or pounds, I can't

remember which – not euros, anyway. They hadn't yet been invented. Whatever it was, that was quite a high price for a camera in those days. I needed a good one, as I was photographing for one of the missionary magazines at the time. It was nothing exceptional, just a good average camera. It was built to last, not as in these fraudulent days of what they call planned obsolescence.'

★

I spent the rest of that summer working as a tour-guide, my knowledge of spoken French helping to secure the job for me. The pay was fairly miserly, but I made a fair bit in tips – I had taken a page from Eoin's book, smiling at people, actually making eye-contact with them, and at least trying to be interested in what interested them. Time and again, I discovered that people did often become interesting – even endearing – if I treated them with the respect of really listening to them.

In September, a few of my old gang from school were going to France on a two-weeks cycling and camping holiday. They tried hard to persuade me to join them – my comparative fluency in the vernacular would have been an advantage from their point of view. I'm sure, though, that there was an element of genuine concern for me as well. My pals realised that I was in pretty low form on account of Eoin. They honestly thought that, if only I could face camping in France again – provided I drank enough beer – they could get me firing on all cylinders once more.

At first, I did not want to go. Then, under heavy pressure, I said 'What the hell!' and made up my mind to tough it out and join them. That resolve held firm until the night before our departure, when I just knew that I could not go through with it. In spite of my best intentions, I would have been like a wet blanket on the whole trip. It would have been a horror story. They all used a lot of bad language, convinced that they could 'cure' me, if only I could be persuaded to take the plunge. When, at last, it became clear that I was beyond their therapeutic skills, they were very decent about it. All the guys hit me – their way of showing affection – and the girls cuddled me in their various catch-as-catch-can holds. It was sort of moving.

Mid-trip, they all signed one of those outrageously vulgar postcards in which the French excel, and sent it to me. I had to lie bare-faced to my mother about what the French text printed on the card actually meant. The lurid illustration should have been enough for her.

In subsequent analysis of my reasons for not going on the trip, I realised that, if there were probably elements of self-pity, morbidity, and the maudlin intermingled with purer motives, the main factor was a deep feeling of unfinished business. I could not bring myself to loll in a tent in France while Eoin's killer was still on the loose. He was the best friend I ever had, and some shit had killed him. And what had I done so far to avenge him? Nothing!

Let there be no loose thinking on that point at least: I *thirsted* for revenge.

CHAPTER ELEVEN

Returning to France at the beginning of October, I made a day trip detour from Paris to Orléans, to talk to Father Fred and to Inspector Péron. I had already sent each of them a letter, giving Father O'Keeffe's valuation of the camera which he had lent to Eoin.

The Inspector, who had kindly come to the monastery to see Fred and myself together, gave expression to what all three of us were thinking: 'This rules out any question of the camera being taken for its intrinsic value. Ten pounds is about a hundred and forty new francs in today's money. The very suggestion that a grey-haired gentleman driving a big black expensive Citrëon car murdered this young man for such a camera is ludicrous. It makes no sense at all.'

We both agreed. Fred took up the running: 'The alternative suggestion is that Eoin had taken some photograph which could incriminate the driver.'

I cut in: 'Eoin was anything but a blackmailer; he would never hold anyone to ransom, if that is what you are saying.'

Fred looked mildly surprised at my vehemence, but said nothing. Even as I was saying those words in Eoin's defence, I remembered, uneasily, how he used to say that drivers would sometimes tell him very private things – even dark secrets. Still, I could not get my head around the idea that he would ever sneak on somebody who had confided in him. I closed my mind to the possibility that he might feel that he had a higher duty to betray a confidence. In the event, I did not say anything at that time about Eoin as a hearer of dark secrets. Perhaps I should have.

The Inspector changed the subject. He told us how many big Citroën cars had been sold in France since 1960. I can't remember the exact figure, but it was in the thousands, not hundreds. Practically all of these cars belonged to grey-headed men who had made their money in business, the professions, politics, or the trade unions. In those days, credit was tight. You simply did not have such a car if you could not afford to pay cash up front for it.

The Inspector drew the appropriate conclusion: 'Don't think that it will be easy to find the grey-haired gentleman who bought a spade in Saumur, and – maybe – buried a body near Bourgueil the same day, and – maybe – drove a large black car which – maybe – was a Citroën. Of the thousands of people who drive big black Citroëns, the vast majority are grey-haired men. We are working on it, of course, but the most I can do is to send documentation to the various regions in France where our records show that there are, or were, big black Citroëns. A chain, as you know, is as strong as its weakest link, and, quite frankly, I cannot guarantee how diligently the search will be conducted. Will alibis be checked rigorously? Besides, most of these grey-haired gentlemen are important, and often powerful, figures in their own communities. Even the police are not immune to being over-awed, and so acting – how shall I say? – in an accommodating manner.'

Taking the train to Strasbourg late that afternoon, I reflected that, realistically, there were limits to what the French police could be expected to do. Left to myself, I thought sourly, I would have had no scruple about locking up all those thousands of grey-headed owners of big black Citroëns on Devil's Island, and depriving them of garlic, pastis, camembert, frogs, snails, and Gauloises until one of them broke down in tears and confessed to Eoin's murder.

★

Alsace – if it has a very cold winter, with snow on the ground for months on end, and a blistering summer, complete with hail stones – does compensate with beautiful seasons of spring and autumn. I tried to get a bit of a holiday and to forget – even temporarily – sadder days and thoughts, by touring with a few friends on the Route aux Vins, to sample *'le vin fou'* – the 'new wine' or, literally, the 'mad wine' – which is a particularly potent kind of alcopop, too sweet to put down, with a kick like a mule. The wines of Alsace have been life-long favourites of mine: Riesling, Sylvaner, Gewurtztraminer, Pinot Noir and Blanc. There is a Chinese proverb which begins, 'If you want to be happy for a day – get drunk.' I managed – never for a day, but certainly for an hour or two – when I could even think about Eoin without pain.

Meanwhile, life went on. I made progress with my research into Maurice Blondel, and felt that I had something new to say about him. I had also met a girl called Marianne, whom I really liked and respected, meaning that – admittedly by *her* decree – we didn't have sex until we were married three years later. Amazingly, she still puts up with me thirty-seven years later. She says that I'm a real creep, but a bit of a laugh. I never know which part to take more seriously. The fact is that to love is always to be astonished, and to be at the same time enormously grateful. Hell must be definitive ingratitude and total predictability. Of course, this is some people's idea of heaven and security.

Marianne, who is from Angolême in the Charente, is a year younger than myself. She was doing a *stage* when I met her, training as a librarian in the Bibliothèque Nationale, on the Place de la République in Strasbourg. In those far-off days, Marianne helped me to 'get over' Eoin's death, or at least grieve creatively, and, ultimately, to let him go. In the end, without ever having known Eoin, she seemed to have grown to love him as much as myself. They have some great qualities in common: total generosity, and being utterly devoid of all envy. They have both made me conscious of something of which there is too little awareness today: that envy – 'the hidden snake bite' – as one ancient writer describes it is simply the most hateful, and also the most self-punishing, vice in a human being. The envious person suffers perpetual built-in torment.

The atmosphere in the university was much better. A lot of the dinosaur professors had got the message, and quietly retired to their 'country estates'. This was by no means a simple question of age. Some of the older men had the courage not to retire, because they had the intelligence and the objectivity to see that they were much more open to change than troglodytes half their age. The students sorted them out quickly enough. In the faculty of Catholic Theology, where I was associated as an *auditeur libre* – which meant that I could come and go as I pleased – one of the oldest professors was greeted with a standing ovation when he bravely stepped onto the rostrum for his first lecture of the new term. He must have known that another member of the faculty, thirty years his junior, had been welcomed with a barrage of catcalls and hissing by the already thin attendance that had bothered to turn up.

I suspect that there were even more radical changes of personnel in the administration of government departments, that had simply kept the lid on a seething cauldron for far too long. One summer vacation had been much too short a time in which to rectify situations that had become endemic – even chronic. But now the students had hope and, above all, the feeling that they were being treated with the respect afforded to adults, that they were being listened to, and that somebody was trying to cope with their real problems. On that basis, they were more than willing to show their own goodwill and to be patient.

The weeks and months passed. It seemed that I had not heard from either Fred or Inspector Péron for ages. I presumed that this meant that the inquiry was running out of steam. It took all of Marianne's common sense and tough love to keep me from getting seriously depressed at this stage.

'What would Eoin say?' she asked.

'He can't say anything because he is dead. That's the whole point,' I replied petulantly.

'I'll tell you what he would say,' she continued, as if she had not heard my peevish reply. 'Eoin would say, "Andrew, stop beating yourself up. I know that you would do anything to dry my tears for the bitter things that happened to me. But you are

125

not God, nor Solomon, nor even Maigret. God has already dried my tears, and I am happy. I want you to be happy, too. Be patient, and, above all, don't let your tyrannical superego trample all over you." That is what Eoin would say.'

She was right, the witch! (She is reading this, of course.) Those are not the words that Eoin would have used, but the mixture of wisdom, tenderness, humour, faith, common sense, and the necessary deflation of my own self-importance, are uncannily the same. I sometimes think that she must have known and loved Eoin in some previous existence.

Then, at last, there was a development: a first suspect turned up. That is, a first suspect apart from myself, which was a pleasant change. I am not sure if they actually arrested the guy at this stage, or merely brought him in for questioning. He was grey-headed and he had been in or near Saumur, with his big black Citroën, on the weekend when Eoin was murdered. In fact, he had stayed in a seedy hotel in the town for two nights – the Friday and the Saturday – where he had given a false name. The shop assistant at the supermarket where the spade had been bought on the Friday morning had failed to pick him out at an identification parade, whether because he was genuinely unable to recognise him, or because the driver of the big black car had thoughtfully greased his palm with five hundred francs. When the bribe was discovered – which it was, because, incredibly, a cheque had changed hands – both men were arrested. The shop assistant was indignantly dismissed from his employment, though perhaps more for being caught than for accepting bribes. His is a trade notorious for sweeteners and backhanders.

The shop assistant was in deep trouble with the police as well as with his employers. He eventually persuaded them that, whereas he was never one to look a gift-horse in the mouth, and so had gratefully received a payment from the grey-haired gentleman, his failure to identify that person as the man to whom he had sold a spade was, in fact, the truth, the whole truth, and nothing but the truth. He was simply not the man, nor did he look even remotely like him.

The gentleman was never charged with Eoin's murder, due to a lack of motive, and because of the reluctant appearance of a married woman who testified that she had kept the grey-headed gentlemen so busy in the seedy hotel in Saumur for the entire weekend that he would have had neither the time, the inclination, nor the energy to murder anyone.

This evidence inspired the adulterer's wife to dump him, realising that, when he was supposed to be in Perpignan drumming up interest in lavatory paper, he was, in fact, misbehaving with some trollop in Saumur. While he did not particularly miss his wife, he did miss her considerable private fortune. The first thing that had to go, as a result, was the big black car, and then – as a knock-on effect, so to speak – the 'trollop' in Saumur.

★

Unlike their German neighbours, the French do not make a big deal over Christmas. Schools and universities only have a short break, with the more substantial holiday being at the beginning of February, rated as mid-year for French academies. I had not been home for Christmas the previous year, and had felt very lonely. It is impossible to carve up Christmas like a turkey: did I miss Silent Night or Jingle Bells, Santa Claus or the Three Wise Men, midnight mass or plum pudding? In other words, was I a Christian or a pagan? Perhaps I was both at the same time. I am no theologian, but it seems to me that this is what the Incarnation is all about: God's compromise with bad taste. In conclusion, I missed Christmas – the whole piece, period – as our American friends would say.

On an impulse, I decided to go home on a flying visit, for just six days, door to door. I knew that my mother would like that. On another impulse, I decided to ask Marianne if she would like to come, and she accepted, never having been in an Anglophone country before. I was not at all sure that my mother would like me to be bringing girls home to stay but had a series of surprises. Firstly, that Marianne could speak English quite well – we had always spoken French together. My second surprise was that my mother offered us – not quite a double bed, but the twin beds in the guest room, which I blushingly declined. Marianne laughed out loud. My third surprise was that my mother and Marianne got on brilliantly. They talked endlessly about everything – their favourite topic being, of course, all the things that were wrong with me.

There were sterner tests to come. I trotted Marianne up and down before the lads like a prize filly, hoping that they would like her, and not think that the French accent was 'a bit of a pain in the backside'. Until the European thing got going in Ireland, Dubliners had a certain number of fixed ideas about language. Firstly, they were convinced that the best correct English was only as spoken by themselves. I think that Swift was responsible for this perverse opinion. Secondly, Dubliners believed that there was something weird, and even comical, about any other language – except Irish, of course. Irish was bracketed with religion, and therefore did you good, though you were not really meant to enjoy it. They certainly thought that there was something wrong with anybody who actually spoke a foreign language, or even spoke English with a 'funny' accent.

I need not have worried. Marianne was unanimously voted as 'great gas' and 'mighty craic'. A friend called Billy Duffy even asked me enviously: 'Jesus, Andy, could you fix me up with one of them French birds?'

The night before we left, my parents invited Eoin's parents over for dinner. They told me that it was their first outing, except to immediate family, since Eoin had died. They managed well and seemed to enjoy themselves, as much as they could with that awful sadness in their hearts.

'We think of him every moment,' his Mum said. Her husband nodded, shielding his eyes.

I walked them home. Eoin's Mum linked arms with me.

'Andrew,' she said, 'Marianne is such a lovely girl. We are so happy for you. She will be a beautiful sister-in-law for Eoin. In fact, I am sure that he sent her to you.'

I was always touched when Eoin's parents spoke of him as my brother. Still, I laughed and said lightly: 'Hey, don't shotgun me into it. We've only just met!'

She laughed in her turn and kissed me, saying almost skittishly: 'Go away with you! You're head over heels in love with her. Of course, you will marry her.'

When we got back to Paris, Marianne took the train to Angoulême to spend a week with her parents, to report on her visit at length, and, no doubt, to reassure the old folks at home that she was not pregnant, and that I was actually a nice boy, with standards. I could not claim, on the basis of my mediocre track record in the area of standards, that this had always been true – far from it. But the miracle of love is that it can recreate people overnight – even a jerk like me.

I did not make the detour to Orléans this time. Fred, I knew, was away visiting foreign missionary stations. I phoned Inspector Péron. Looking back, he was probably genuinely not available. I felt, however, that he had become cautious as a result of the previous débacle that had uncovered, not murder, but a squalid love-nest. It seemed fairly sure that I would not be hearing from the Inspector again until he was on surer ground.

I found Strasbourg in the grip of a massive freeze-up, with heavy snowfall which would last several weeks. Cars all had chains fitted to their tyres, making them better able to grip onto the snow. Snowploughs kept the main thoroughfares clear. Most intriguing of all, there seemed to be a law which obliged riparian owners to keep the expanse of pavement fronting their properties free from snow. Old gentlemen, unmistakably of the haute bourgeoisie, could be seen outside, wielding shovels and spades from half past six in the morning, and making a good job of it.

I spent a day, from time to time, skiing in the Vosges with like-minded friends. The ski pistes there are modest, and tend to run out of snow, but it was a good year; it took my mind off sad thoughts and loneliness. Besides, I found, to my surprise, that I was a good skier. Other things I am good at include wriggling out of tackles in rugby, and dancing. I think there must be some connection. The way you use your hips and your ass is vital in all three choreographies. I had a rugby coach in school who used to shout from the side-lines, 'Use your ass, man!' He was American-trained, and proud of it. Eventually, the Head Brother had to tell him to desist. Apparently, it was not setting 'the right tone' for a prestigious school, whose founder, we were frequently told, was a hot tip for being proclaimed a saint some-day soon. He hasn't managed it yet. Perhaps the Pope has heard about what the coach was yelling at the lads from the side-lines.

One morning early in the New Year, I was dashing out the door to travel to Entzheim, which is the domestic airport for Strasbourg. Marianne was travelling back in style from Angoulême. Some local delegation had chartered a plane for an official visit to the Council of Europe, and was selling off a few spare seats for a song. Marianne was fortunate to get one of these. When I had actually seen how lonely I had been without her for all of a whole week, I realised the truth of what Eoin's Mum had said. Yes, indeed, I was head over heels in love with Marianne!

On my way through the hall, the concierge – that curious French combination of porter, receptionist, and controller of student morality – handed me a package that had arrived that morning in the post. It was from the university, and, I thought, probably contained one of these interminable forms to be filled in for my scholarship from *La Ville de Strasbourg*. I opened it in the airport bus. It contained another packet with a covering letter. The letter said that the enclosed packet had arrived to the university 'some weeks before'. As I would see, the letter continued, the packet had been rather vaguely addressed and had ended up in the professors' common room, in a pigeonhole reserved for the mail of guest lecturers, where it had languished for several weeks, enticing no takers. Eventually, it was Monsignor Nédoncelle, who was helping me with my thesis, who had suggested that I might be the intended recipient.

I turned my attention to the enclosed packet. It had been posted in Paris in mid-November. It was addressed, in block capitals, to:

Monsieur L'Abbé Olden André,
Palais de l'Université,
67 Strasbourg, Bas-Rhin

I burst out laughing. The name was a reasonable frenchify-ing of my own. The inversion did not surprise me, because peo-ple often mistook my first and my family name, and, anyhow, the French often reverse names on envelopes. But whoever thought that I was a priest – Monsieur l'Abbé – was in serious need of counselling. The addition of Bas-Rhin was not neces-sary, 67 being sufficient to identify the *département*. I guessed that this was something that somebody either anxious or else not very intelligent might write to compensate for the vague-ness of the rest of the address.

I set to work on this inner package. It consisted of a large brown envelope folded around a stiff card pouch, such as often contain travel tickets or photographs. It was quite difficult to open without a scissors, because of the copious use of sellotape going in every direction. Once again – I thought – a sign of anxiety or scrupulosity. Halfway through undoing this awk-ward bundle, I became conscious that one entire edge of what-ever it contained had been subjected to extensive burning.

At some point before I had finally untangled the mess, I somehow guessed what the packet contained. I was so startled that, for the first time in about twenty years, I nearly wet myself. It could not be! I told myself, half afraid to go on. But I did go on – and indeed it *was*. I was staring at eighteen photographs of our ill-fated camping trip together – taken, undoubtedly, by Eoin's camera. They had been sent to me personally, 'Olden André'. Whatever about the inversion of the names, the French spelling, the ludicrous Monsieur L'Abbé, there could be no doubt that I was the intended recipient.

The bottom third of each photograph was shrivelled by fire. On the outside of the pouch containing the photos, there were several dirty welts, consistent with somebody beating it vigorously with a stick or a poker – no doubt in order to extinguish the fire that had been consuming the pouch and its contents.

My mind jolted sickeningly into overdrive. What did it all mean? I clutched and half-glanced at the photographs, trying to take them in by fistfuls all together – some of them upside down or back to front, clawing at them feverishly, all thumbs, dropping one or two – and then more – when I lunged clumsily to scrape them off the floor of the lurching bus.

Who had stolen Eoin's camera off his body? The murderer, obviously. Who had sent me these photographs? The murderer? It must be! Why had he done that? To mock me? To warn me?

And who had tried to burn the photographs? The murderer? So, he first tried to destroy the photographs. And then, what? Why did he change his mind and fish them out of the flames again? Was it because the killer had second thoughts, and realised that it would be much more fun to scare the living daylights out of me, to put the heart across me, to torture me?

Or did somebody else snatch the photographs from the fire, beat them with the poker to quench them, and then send them to me? And why would anyone do that?

My head was bursting with shreds of half-formulated and grotesquely inconsistent ideas. What seemed clear was that somebody had singled me out, Andrew Olden, or Olden André, and had made personal to me what had happened to Eoin. Was this a threat or a warning? Did it mean that I, too, was in danger? Where had this person – whoever he was – got my name? That could only be from Eoin himself. When he was travelling in that big black car, he had probably blabbed happily all about me, and how we were hitch-hiking around the country together.

Perhaps, unknown to Eoin – the least suspicious person that

God ever made – that driver was some nut-case who hated all Irish people, or Catholics, or students, or ex-Scouts, or God alone knows who or what. I was trying to think of all the things that Eoin and I had in common and that some lunatic could conceivably loathe. But, even in my agitated frame of mind, I had to recognise that nobody – but nobody – is so crazy as to seek out and murder people for such far-fetched reasons as what Eoin and I had in common. People have been killed – and in great numbers – because they were Jews, or Poles, or Tutsis, or Christians, or Igbos, or Kurds, or Muslims. But this is always in the context of a pogrom, a collective madness, a mass diabolical possession.

Or maybe – and here I was again, off on another tack – just maybe we were back in a variation of Mister Nasty Bastard's favourite scenario, where some fanatic had got the wrong idea about the relationship between Eoin and myself? Could that be why Eoin had been murdered? And was that why the camera had been taken off his dead body? To identify Eoin's companion, then to gloat over me, and to threaten me – just when I was beginning to get over his death and to feel 'safe'. Was this to tell me that there would be no forgiveness for what this crazy killer thought that we had done together, and that I, too, was going to die – and deserved to die – because of it?

Even drowning in this witch's cauldron of swirling and conflicting ideas, I was lucid about a few things. First of all – with all my faults and failings – I am not a coward. If there was really some mean-minded creep out there who had got it in for me – well, 'Make my day', as the tough guy says in the movies. I would have done my level best to spoil his fun.

So, deep down, what was really upsetting me? Why was I so patently over-reacting? I can only offer an explanation that has come into focus for me over the years – I do think that this was the real cause of my feelings of sheer anger, and, at the same time, of helplessness.

The fact is that I would probably prefer to be gay than to be celibate, not for the sex – which, quite frankly, bewilders me – but for the intimacy with some other human person that such a relationship implies. The *other* fact is that, during those few weeks together – as I have already said – I had come to have a deep respect for Eoin's celibacy. I do believe that he was being driven by the Spirit to play for very high stakes: either total integrity, total fidelity to his vocation, total generosity – or else to become a cheat, a hypocrite, or a crabbed body-hating misogynist. And Eoin was none of those things.

So, to be fair to myself, I didn't give a tinker's curse what some crazy shit-head might think or say about me. But I did care, and I do still feel compelled to give testimony to what and who Eoin was. It angered me intensely that his life could be snuffed out, wasted, by fanatical hatred and for a futile lie. My dominant emotion each time I was reminded what had happened to my friend was not fear of what might also happen to myself: it was impotent rage at what had happened to *him*.

When Marianne emerged, on time, from her flight, we hugged. She knew immediately that there was something wrong.

'Andrew, you are hyperventilating!'

I said, 'Of course, I'm so excited to see you again.' Then I spoiled everything – to my intense embarrassment – by dissolving into tears.

In the bus back into town from the airport, we held hands and talked in whispers about the photographs, and about the sudden turmoil that they had unleashed in my soul. We decided not to look at them immediately, but to have a nice lunch, and then to go through them carefully together. When we got to Marianne's apartment, she went out for a few moments and came back with a small pill which she ordered me to take. I have never been a pill-popper – a few paracetamol for a cold or a hangover would be my limit. I took it obediently, then inquired what it was.

'Strychnine', Marianne answered, and kissed me.

'So this is goodbye', I joked bleakly.

She kissed me again, and said: 'No, not until you pay for my lunch. It is valium. The girl upstairs eats them.'

I got worried, so Marianne added, 'There is no fear of you, Andrew. That's one of your good points. You will never be a substance-abuser. But just now, you have gone off the deep end. We have got to get you back and able to function.'

She added, in English, an Irish expression which she had probably learnt from my mother – about me: 'You have gone with the fairies!'

We went to a little restaurant in the Avenue de la Robertsau, which we both loved, and could afford occasionally. Between the meal, the valium, and Marianne, I was feeling much better after lunch. Back in Marianne's apartment, we spread out the photographs on the kitchen table. We were careful to preserve the order, though I would have had little difficulty in restoring it, as it followed the chronology of our trip.

There were three shots of Eoin himself, where he had asked someone else to hold the camera. One of these, which I had taken myself, was of Eoin and the three Canadian girls at Versailles; another was of himself and me with the two girls at Huelgoat, before things had begun to go so badly wrong. The third was at Saumur, probably the night before Eoin embarked on the journey from which he was never to return. I cannot say who took this photograph, and I have no recollection of how it came to be taken. It was unique in the collection, as being a head-and-shoulders portrait of a single person. Miraculously, though it had been damaged in the fire like the rest of them, the essentials were intact. Every feature was clear and beautiful. I don't exaggerate if I say that Eoin looked like the Archangel Michael, except that, inevitably, he was always smiling. When I eventually succeeded in retrieving the photographs from the police, I took this one to the most talented portrait-painter I knew, who painted me an inspired copy in oils of the original. It has been hanging on my study wall ever since. Even after all these years, I talk to Eoin sometimes.

The first photo in the series, taken on day one of our trip, was a sneak view of me, trying out my prototype auto-stopping technique. I looked like a cross between Bluebeard and Count Dracula, randy for a bit of what he fancied. You would need to have a virulent death-wish to take me into your car. The last three photographs were two taken of the community in Orléans, when Eoin was visiting, and – the very last one of all – of a big black car, seemingly shot in haste from the back, as it pulled up to take Eoin aboard. Were it not for the valium, the lunch, and Marianne, I would probably have begun to hyper-ventilate all over again.

'Are you thinking the same thing as me?' Marianne asked.

'Yes, this is the murderer's car. It is the same big black car that was seen by some local when and where Eoin was actually being buried.'

Marianne nodded, and then shook her head.

'Oui – mais!' she said, agreeing and demurring at the same time. 'Why is Eoin photographing that car? It is not a very interesting shot.'

'That is true,' I conceded. ' I suppose he just wanted a complete record of our trip. So the first photo shows me not stopping a car – and the last shot shows Eoin just having landed one.'

'Perfect!' Marianne continued, with just a trace of sarcasm. 'Eoin knew when he took his first photo that it was his first photo. Are you suggesting that he knew that this last one was to be his last photo? Those films have space for twenty-four, even thirty-six shots, and we have only eighteen. So how did he know that this was to be the last one?'

I did not answer, because I couldn't. It was Marianne who spoke again.

'So, this is the man who killed Eoin,' she said, picking up the photograph from the table. 'It is certainly taken after he has visited his community in Orléans, and when he was on his way back to Saumur – perhaps an hour or less before he died.'

'Sweet Jesus!' I groaned. 'Yes – well, we can't actually see the killer, but we have just got to read off the registration number of his car, and we have the shit cold. Quick, show me!'

'*Hélas!*' Marianne answered. 'That is just the part that has been burnt off – look!'

She handed me the photograph.

'Oh fuck!' I said with feeling.

'*S'il te plaît?*'

I had to explain myself. I said that this was an expression one used when one was experiencing extreme frustration. I also warned her that it was not a lady-like thing to say – which it was not, as recently as the last millennium.

Later, back at my apartment, I rang Inspector Péron from the communal telephone booth, next to the concierge's lair on the ground floor. The concierge, a most unlovely person called Madame Blum, took a blatant interest in all telephone calls in French or Alsatian, and was visibly resentful when I spoke in English. I had to speak in French to the Inspector, so I was fairly brief. He was very excited to hear about the photographs.

'I'll post them to you tomorrow,' I offered magnanimously – but getting in a firm stipulation that I wanted those photographs back. Ignoring that part of my conversation, he replied to my first proposal.

'No, don't post them, Andrew. Please wrap the photographs up exactly as you received them – inner envelope, outer envelope, covering letter, the lot – and enclose them in a strong paper carrier bag. Then bring them to the Préfecture de Police, in the Avenue de la Forêt Noire, addressed clearly to myself. Ask for Inspector Garnier. I will have contacted him in the meanwhile. He will deliver the package to me safely by special police courier. I will be in touch with you in about a week's time, hopefully with a progress report.'

I followed the Inspector's instructions the next day.

CHAPTER TWELVE

True to his word, Inspector Péron contacted me ten days after I had deposited Eoin's photographs at the Préfecture in Strasbourg. He did it in a way that probably aroused the concierge's interest, and her worst suspicions. He sent a squad car around to collect me and bear me away. In Madame Blum's book that could only mean one thing: that I was in deep trouble with the police. I knew from what I had been told by others – mostly by my garrulous grocer – that Madame had quite a track record when it came to coping with the police in various forms and uniforms.

Alsace had not just been occupied by the Third Reich during the Second World War, it had been annexed. The concierge, I was given to understand by malicious informants (who clearly detested her), had received regular calls from the Gestapo, in search of Jews, homosexuals, gypsies, and other undesirables who, according to Nazi doctrine, did not deserve to live. Impeccably uniformed and icily well mannered, with much saluting and clicking of heels, these bloodhounds were thorough, and entirely ruthless. The concierge, admittedly, found herself between a rock and a hard place. Whatever her personal sympathies might be – on the doubtful assumption that she had any – she had sold the pass several times.

There was one particularly sickening case involving a family group of a grandmother and five small children. These were Polish Jews who had fled to France from the murderous Nazi pursuit of their people, which had begun in earnest once the Eastern front had been opened up in the early forties.

Initially, the Germans had shown some restraint in respect of French native Jews. But there was already a strong vein of anti-semitism among the far-right nationalist supporters of Marshal Pétain, the French puppet head-of-state. When it became clear that neither the Christian churches nor even French Jewish organisations were prepared to speak out in defence of foreign Jews, the Gestapo resumed their hideous project of mass-murder with gusto. Some people told me that Madame Blum voluntarily betrayed this elderly woman and her five little grandchildren. Others said that she only did what she had to do to avoid being shot herself for failing to report that she was harbouring foreign Jews.

The fact is that by mid-July 1942, thirteen thousand immigrant Jews had already been arrested in France and were destined for the gas-chamber at Auschwitz. This worn-out and half-starved old woman and the five children whom she was trying desperately to protect were dragged from the single room which they had been occupying on the top floor of Madame Blum's premises and sent to the *Vél d'Hiv*, a bicycle-racing stadium near the already grossly overcrowded collection camp at Drancy. There were as many as eight thousand Jews crammed into this stadium, which had a glass roof, resulting in midday temperatures in July as high as 40 degrees C. Apart from the overcrowding and the merciless heat, there were zero facilities – no bedding, only one water tap for eight thousand people, not a single lavatory – and the five cubicles that could have been used were securely locked because they had windows that could conceivably have served as escape routes out of the stadium. There was no food or drink except one or two cups of soup each day. The pathetic little family huddled there for four or five days, during which time the old lady and the second-youngest child died of excessive hardship and sheer misery.

The other four children were then moved to a hospital, from where they were sent to Auschwitz on August 24 1942, together with more than five hundred other sick children and adolescents. All those youngsters – their ages ranged from two to seventeen years old – were murdered by gassing the same day as they arrived in the camp.

After the war, a lot of people in Alsace – as indeed elsewhere in France – had to keep quiet about what they had done, or not done, and about what they had seen or heard. Perhaps few families had not had to compromise in some way or, at the very least, had looked the other way at certain times. What makes Madame Blum's collaboration all the more gut-wrenching, and possibly pathetic, is the fact that Blum is often a Jewish name.

Inspector Péron's motives for sending a squad car to fetch me were simpler and less sinister than Blum had been accustomed to during the war. He knew that I had no telephone in my apartment, and that I was uncomfortable about using the common telephone booth for sensitive conversations, if they had to be in French. He wanted an extended and candid discussion with me – for my information, but also for his own – so he was going to phone me at the Préfecture, where I could sit down privately and in reasonable comfort, and have the space and the time to concentrate and to think.

Péron was a really excellent policeman, because he was thoughtful in both senses of the word: in himself, and also for the well-being of other people. That, I have found in my own life, is a sure-fire formula for people who need to understand what is really going on around them.

And so it was that I was soon comfortably seated in the office of a cheerful Inspector, who brightly said, 'Well, I'm going home to plant some bulbs. Let yourself out when you're finished.' He then got Péron on the line, and left me on my own.

Péron said that he had got Father Fred beside him, who could also speak on some sort of primitive party line. We all said 'Hello' or '*Bonjour*' to each other, and the Inspector began his report.

'According to the experts, the outer envelope containing your correspondence was probably written by a middle-aged woman, of modest intelligence, so, therefore, not by the murderer, who was most likely a strong man, of ruthless intelligence and determination.

'Second point. This woman is probably living in some place where the newspaper *La Dépêche du Midi* circulates. That is to say, in the southern part of France. "Why?" you may ask. Because she addresses you as Monsieur l'Abbé.'

'You've lost me,' I exclaimed. 'I don't understand at all.'

'Ahha, I will explain,' the Inspector assured me. '*La Dépêche* likes crime – or likes writing about it. Understandably. One of the most active directors is René Bousquet. The name probably means nothing to you, but he was the Chief of Police during most of the war. He is a controversial figure – I'll say no more about that – except that he has strong views about crime. Accordingly, his newspaper reported your poor friend's murder extensively. They made inquiries at the campsite in Saumur. That is where they got your name. We – I mean the police – did not give it to them. Your name is recorded in the camp site register exactly in the form that it appeared in *La Dépêche* – 'Olden André' – and that is precisely what is written on the package sent to you. Plus, they were also told at the campsite that you and Eoin were two priests from the *Séminaire International*, who were both working in Strasbourg University.'

'Holy God,' I interjected, 'how inaccurate can you get? Eoin usually did the registrations, because he often arrived at the campsite before me. He must have given his own address, and they assumed that mine was the same. I've certainly never been called a priest before!'

I said the word 'priest' as if it were something outlandish to call anyone.

Fred laughed.

I had completely forgotten that he was eavesdropping. Embarrassed, I said sheepishly, 'Sorry, Father!'

The priest laughed again. '*Il n'y a pas de quoi!*' he reassured me pleasantly.

'Such inaccuracies are very important,' the Inspector resumed. 'You see how they help us to establish the truth. The person who addressed the envelope to you as Monsieur l'Abbé almost certainly got your name and inaccurate details from *La Dépêche du Midi*. Arguably, and indeed probably, that person – that middle-aged woman of modest intelligence – is living herself in *Le Midi*, in the southern half of our *chère patrie*. So, that is another brick in the edifice that we are trying to construct.

But let us turn to the question of the car. First of all, it is a

Renault, not a Citroën. So, we shall have to start that part of the inquiry all over again. It is frustrating that the fire has destroyed the most vital piece of information – the number plate on the car. If we had that, we could be making an arrest before the sun went down. But, at least, the grey-haired, made-man profile of the killer remains probably true. These cars are roughly in the same price bracket, meaning that I, for instance, could not afford either of them.'

Fred spoke. 'Who is this middle-aged woman, who lives in the South of France, reads *La Dépêche du Midi*, and also has access to the photographs that Eoin took with the camera which was stolen off his dead body?'

The Inspector answered. 'First of all, what is her motive? I think she is trying to help us, and yet fears to be discovered. A middle-aged woman goes well with a grey-haired killer. Might they not be man and wife? One possible scenario is that he threw the photos into the fire, and she – when his back was turned – fished them out again and sent them to Andrew.'

'Well, I am glad to have them,' I said, 'even in their messed-up condition. But there is nothing incriminating in these photographs, so why did the killer steal the camera, and why did he go to the trouble of developing the film? And, above all else, why did he murder Eoin?'

'We can have theories about all these questions, but they are just that: theories and not yet facts. But, *'petit à petit l'oiseau fait son nid'* – little by little, the bird makes its nest. The important thing is that we have made progress. Let's hope that we can keep up the momentum.'

The Inspector thanked me courteously for having sent him the photographs. He said that he hoped that I would get them back – eventually. I did get them back – very eventually. He did warn me that there would inevitably be '*des chinoiseries*', which is a dynamic equivalent for red tape. There were.

★

The Inspector had been wrong about one thing. He thought that the name of René Bousquet, one of the directors of the *Dépêche du Midi*, would mean nothing to me. But it did. I had been told that Bousquet, as Chief of Police, had personally organised the Rafle du Vel d'Hiv, the round-up of Jews into that stinking stadium where that old woman and all of her five little grandchildren had begun the journey that had ended in them losing their lives. How strange that such a man should have been even indirectly involved in helping to find Eoin's killer. Or rather . . . I had a strange, and totally irrational, intuition that it was that elderly Jewish woman and her five little grandchildren, who had lived and suffered in the same house as myself, who were helping me to find Eoin's murderer.

To finish with Bousquet, he had very powerful political protectors after the war and made a successful career in banking and newspapers. Finally indicted for crimes against humanity as late as 1991, he was shot dead by Christian Didier on 8 June 1993, weeks before his trial was due to begin.

★

I slept badly that night. I could not shake off the feeling that there was something I was missing. A phrase floated into my mind, bubbling up from my subconscious. It was, 'the cart before the horse', and it kept bothering me like a dull toothache. I finished up shouting it out loud like an incantation or an exorcism. Something was just out of focus, like when you have forgotten a name which you should definitely remember. At moments, you nearly have it – and then it slips through your fingers again.

I appeared at Marianne's apartment at eight o'clock in the morning.

'*Nom d'une pipe*,' she exclaimed. 'It is my day off. I was having a lie-in. I am barely decent. Come in anyhow. Is something wrong?'

I answered, as if the slippery fish of the thought that was obsessing me was self-explanatory, 'the cart is before the horse' and added by way of further elucidation, 'Interrogate me – under torture if necessary?'

'Are you looking for kinky sex – at this hour of the morning?' my true-love replied.

I burst out laughing.

'No,' I said, as we went into the kitchen, 'I promised, no sex until we're married. It's killing me, but at least it proves I really love you: I wouldn't do it for anyone else! But no. What I need is breakfast and brainstorming.'

We sat at the kitchen table, drinking café-au-lait out of bowls, in which we dipped hunks of bread and jam. Americans would call it a working breakfast. We brainstormed. We did not have the photographs under our eyes, but Marianne, in her methodical librarian's way, had listed them chronologically, with short identifying titles that I had supplied. I had asked her to do this – to be sure that we got them all back from the police, but, so soon after parting with the photographs, we both remembered them quite well. Our brainstorming consisted of staring intently at each successive title, with clenched teeth and furrowed brows, willing it to divulge its secrets. We were halfway through this fruitless procedure when I lost my patience and said a rude word.

Marianne laughed and replied, 'We are constipated – I mean mentally constipated. Let's change the methodology of our research. Let's try woman's intuition.'

I raised an incredulous eyebrow and retorted ungraciously.

Marianne ignored my dyspeptic remark – a tactic that has long since been a feature of our happy marriage – and went on.

'Is it a question of a cart before the horse, or is it a horse before the cart? I think it is the last photograph that we should be looking at. Woman's intuition tells me: it is all wrong.'

'What's all wrong about it?' I demanded scornfully.

'I don't know,' she said, maddeningly.

And we got no further than that.

It was during a telephone conversation the next day with Inspector Péron that something clicked in my brain.

'I think I was wrong about the last photograph in the series. I assumed that Eoin took that photo when the motorist was pulling in to take him into his car. That could still be true. Normally, by the time a motorist sees a hitch-hiker and decides to pick him up, he has actually gone past him. He needs time to slow down and stop. So, practically always, the motorist is twenty or thirty yards ahead of the hitch-hiker by the time he has pulled in and come to a halt. Yes, the photo *could* have been taken at that stage. But, on reflection, that is actually unlikely. Psychologically, the back-packer will be much more inclined to shoulder his rucksack and run up and secure his lift than to dawdle over taking photographs, especially if he has to fish his camera out of a pouch looped to his belt.'

'So what are you suggesting now?' the Inspector asked.

'Suppose that the photograph was taken, not when Eoin was

getting into the car, but after he had got out of it – and when the car was pulling away.'

'Well, does it really matter whether it was taken before or after? At least we know now that the car was a Renault and not a Citroën. So, we are working with that.'

'Yes, it does matter,' I insisted. 'If that photo was taken *after* Eoin got out of that car, at last we have a plausible motive for why he was killed.'

There was a silence. Then the Inspector said: 'I'm sorry, you've lost me. What "plausible motive" have we got?'

'Listen, let's say that Eoin, the moment he got out of that car, takes a photo of it, in haste. That photo was obviously taken in haste; it's wobbly.'

'That's true,' the Inspector conceded, 'but, so what?'

'And supposing the driver sees what Eoin is doing in his rear mirror, so he jumps out of his car and kills him?'

The Inspector made one of these rude noises with his mouth that the French are addicted to, and said: 'Is that your "plausible motive?" He kills the boy because he takes a snap of the backside of his car? *Mon Dieu!* I don't think that this is particularly likely.'

'No,' I shot back, 'he does not kill him because he is taking a picture of the back of his car; he kills him because he knows that Eoin is photographing his registration number.'

There was no rude noise this time, but a long silence, and then, with what just might have been interest – or even respect: And why is he doing that?'

'So that he can give the number to the police – maybe. And the driver realises what he is doing and why he is doing it.'

'You mean . . . '

'I mean . . . '

I told the Inspector what Eoin had told me about the readiness of people to confide in him – even sometimes to confess their darkest secrets because, in some way, he represented God, or the hope of understanding or forgiveness. I felt almost silly saying these things. Above all, I thought that the way I was explaining them was so bad that it made Eoin appear like some holier-than-thou nerd and a smug bastard. But, to my surprise, the Inspector did not snort or sigh. Indeed he seemed to understand what I was saying. He raised an unexpected difficulty.

'A priest never tells what he has heard in confession: the driver must have known that he was quite safe.'

'But Eoin was not a priest – not yet anyhow.'

'Yes, I know, but I am sure that he was the kind of chap who would have respected a confidence. And, anyhow, what could somebody have told him that would be worth killing for?'

'God only knows, Inspector. But supposing the guy had told him that he was a raging paedophile, or a serial killer, or a terrorist on his way to do something frightful, you know – that he was somebody really out of control or over the top – Eoin might have thought – he even *should* have thought, I would say – that you guys would really need to hear about what he was hearing. So, that is why he took this photo, and that is why he paid with his life for doing just that.'

There was a pause. Then the Inspector said: 'Actually, I had already worked out that this last photograph was probably taken when Eoin was leaving the car, rather than when he was entering it. Why? Because the car is obviously making a diagonal for the crown of the road, and not for the right side, as it would have been if the driver was pulling in to take a passenger. But – I congratulate you – you have gone much further than I had gone. What you say is no more than a hypothesis, at this stage anyhow, but it is an intriguing hypothesis. I will think long and hard about it.'

CHAPTER THIRTEEN

During the February break, I decided to spend five days in the Vosges at the shrine of Mont Sainte-Odile. It was not that I had caught religion – not exactly anyhow – but I did feel the need to unpack all that had happened to me, for better or for worse, over the last half-year or more. First of all, there had been the Student Revolution. From one point of view, that was a bit of a laugh, and yet we students sensed that nothing would ever be precisely the same again in France, or even in our own lives. It is a banality, but true, nonetheless, that events do shape what we become.

Then there had been those last few precious weeks in Eoin's company. Here was a chap whom I had known all my life, and liked much more than I realised – which means, I suppose, that in the casual way of young people, I had taken him absolutely for granted. Just when I was discovering his depth, quality, and sheer attractiveness, he was callously murdered, practically under my very nose. I had never experienced anything so devastating in my life before. I did the only thing that I could do under the circumstances. I went into automatic pilot, and I managed to function – even quite well. But the wound and shock of Eoin's death had not healed; I knew that. Perhaps it would never heal. Perhaps I did not want it to heal. Is that not what mourning is all about? I am sure that Eoin's parents mourned him until the day they died.

Against that tragic background, the coming of Marianne into my life was like dawn after the darkest night. I would like to believe that Eoin's mum was right when she said that he had sent her to me. I knew, too, that I had changed over the last eight months. If I could not claim to be a better person, I was certain that I had nevertheless been forced to go deeper within myself. What I had discovered was that – between the rough and the smooth – some kind of providence was educating me, moulding my life or – as my personalist philosophers would like to say – shaping my becoming. What did I want to do with my life? What in my deepest heart did I desire? For the first time in my conscious experience I was perhaps beginning to be able to confront those questions. That is what I was trying to do at Mont Sainte-Odile.

Don't get me wrong. The place is an abbey, founded in the seventh century and restored in the seventeenth. It is a place of pilgrimage for all of Alsace. But that does not mean that I was sleeping on bare boards, surviving on a diet of bread and water, and creeping around the place in sackcloth and ashes, barefoot, mumbling the seven penitential psalms. Quite the contrary – I had a comfortable and well-heated room, with a staggering view over the snow-capped mountains. I was fed three times a day on nourishing and plentiful food, including excellent Alsatian wine (Sylvaner) and beer (Mutzig this time). Though I was welcome to attend the various religious ceremonies in the chapel –

which I sometimes did – I was also free to range far and wide in the forests and on the hills, communing with nature, and thinking my own long thoughts.

One day in mid-week, another guest at the abbey drove a few of us over to visit the *Haut-Koenigsbourg* at Orschwiller, near Sélestat. Perched on the massive ridge of the Staufenberg, overlooking the Rhine Valley, this splendid fortress looks like something out of Disneyland or Harry Potter, though it predates both and might easily have inspired either. An original castle on the same site, dating to the fifteenth century, was destroyed during the Thirty Years War. After the Franco-Prussian War (1870), when Alsace was ceded to the German Reich, Kaiser Bill tried hard to get the Alsatians to love him – and all things German – by rebuilding their castle, pretty much as it had been.

The Kaiser used to spend quite a lot of time pottering around at the *Haut-Koenigsberg*. He was vaguely well-disposed towards people, as were they to him. He was, in fact, quite an amiable old buffer. The only drawback was that one of his muddle-headed expansionist fantasies was, at least partially, responsible for the deaths of millions of people in the tragic lunacy of the First World War. One of my fellow tourists claimed to have seen, written on a chimney-piece in the royal apartments, some words in German, equivalent to 'Oops, that's not at all what I had in mind'. My friend maintained that this was written in the Kaiser's own hand and was his disarming way of saying self-deprecatingly 'Silly old me!' to the multitudes of people who had been slaughtered in that cruellest of wars.

When the French eventually got Alsace back again in 1918, they affected to despise the *Haut-Koenigsberg* as the merest vulgar kitsch. But money talks, and when Kaiser Bill's new old pile rapidly became a major tourist attraction, the French did a volte-face, and shamelessly promoted what they had declared to be an unseemly monstrosity to the rank of a national monument.

Meanwhile Kaiser Wilhelm II – to give him his proper title – abdicated in 1918 and went to live in the Netherlands, where he died at the ripe old age of eighty-two in 1941. By then, Adolf Hitler was up to the same tricks as himself – only much worse. As far as I know, the two men never met, probably because the Kaiser thought that Hitler was a common little man – which, of course, he was – and no better than he ought to be. Perhaps it is some indication of the Kaiser's attitude to the whole Nazi obscenity that, when in May 1940, Field-Marshal von Bock, a fervent monarchist himself, drove to Doorn to pay his respects to the former emperor, he was curtly refused entry to the presence.

I did a lot of walking and thinking during those days, and – I suppose – some of it was praying of a sort. I felt Eoin and his parents very close to me, as well as my own, and I knew that my darling Marianne was smiling at me too. At night, I slept soundly and had the most beautiful dreams. I could not remember any of them the next day, but I woke up each morning feeling peaceful and happy. Pleasant dreams have always been, in my life, a sure sign of psychic healing.

On the last day of my retreat – I suppose I could call it that – I wrote a poem, which is something I have done not more than perhaps half a dozen times in my life. A poem is another kind of dream. It just comes out of you, in spite of yourself. Poetry is dangerous. You can work on a poem, but you cannot really filter it through your brain. A poem can let cats out of bags, which is probably why I write so little poetry, and also why I am not sharing this poem with you. It's too 'monkish' in flavour. Not, of course, that I have ever wanted to be a monk. God forbid! After all, that was Eoin's story, wasn't it? Unless, perhaps, Eoin was my own better self – the Narziss to my Goldmund. I wonder if such things are possible?

I got back to Strasbourg late on a Friday afternoon. I knew that Marianne was planning to be away that weekend at a librarians' witches sabbath in Basel. So, no chance of scrounging my supper off her and, more importantly, no chance of even seeing her lovely self for two and a half days, which is sixty hours, and I know precisely how many minutes – because I worked it out – and how many seconds, as well.

One of the good resolutions I had made during my few days communing with nature (or perhaps myself) was to do more walking. I walked with my small suitcase from the bus station to the Esplanade, where I had supper in the student restaurant. I got into a bloodthirsty game of ping-pong with a Mexican chap whom I knew slightly. He beat me soundly, and I paid for his beer.

I got home to my apartment building at about nine o'clock, checked on my postbox in the entrance hall, and went up to my two and a half rooms on the top floor. The minute I opened the door – even before turning on the light – I knew that something was not right. The room was in pitch darkness, and even though it was nothing I saw, nothing seemed to have been disturbed. But somebody had been in that room: I sensed it. I think it was a smell. A very faint hint of what? Deodorant, after-shave lotion, an ointment, not a perfume or a medical thing, not a cosmetic – at least, not a feminine one.

I opened closets at random and pulled out drawers. I was quickly convinced that the apartment had been thoroughly searched. It had been carefully, even cunningly, done. I am a tidy person by nature, and I notice even minor deviations from my anal-retentive standards of neatness – at least, that is what Marianne disobligingly calls them. One of the ways that she has undoubtedly sanctified me over the years is by never leaving anything, to the millimetre, exactly as I have left it. On that Friday evening, I became quite certain that my rooms had been systematically gone over with a fine comb, and I continued to find small tell-tale signs of this trawl for the next several days: clothes folded not quite the right way, books upside down on my desk, a window opened to a notch that I never used. I could even spot that the mattress on my bed had been moved – presumably to see if there was anything under it. How did I know? Simple. I always fold the bottom sheet over the top of the mattress, first, and then tuck in the sides. The intruder had done it exactly the other way.

Nothing had been taken. There was an envelope containing five hundred francs in cash for books that I had ordered lying on the desk. It had not been touched. The reason for the search was not crass acquisitiveness.

In the morning, I talked to the concierge, trying hard not to make it seem like I was accusing her of anything. That was quite difficult *not* to do – I had to assume that only she had another key to my apartment. My delicacy was wasted on the desert air. Madame Blum launched herself immediately into a high screech-owl rejoinder – offensive and defensive at the same time. Was I accusing her? Nobody had been given the key to my rooms. Nobody had been in there. The whole thing was an invention of my own imagination or indeed downright lies, motivated by ill-will and malice.

'Methinks the lady doth protest too much', said Shakespeare, hitting the nail on the head once again. That is precisely what I

methought as well. The only thing I retained from a thoroughly unpleasant interview was the conviction that it was not simply a question of somebody having borrowed the key to my
room without Blum being aware of it. I now felt sure that she
was in on the skulduggery herself, up to her tonsils. Was it *she*
who had searched my room so thoroughly? The very thought of
her rummaging through my personal belongings made my flesh
creep.

Upstairs again, I set myself to wondering why Madame
Blum would search my room or give someone else the key to
search it. What could any such person be looking for? In so far
as I could discover, nothing was missing. I toyed for about five
seconds with the notion that somebody had wanted a sneak
preview of my draft thesis on Blondel. Then I burst out laughing at the sheer arrogance of such an idea. As for my black
diaries or other secret papers: they simply did not exist. Having
racked my brains, I had to admit that neither my accommodation nor I myself would have the slightest interest in a thief or a
snoop who was not excited by the little cash I had, or my passport, or any item in my less-than-trendy wardrobe. In other
words – at least in terms of my few possessions – I was a completely boring person. So why had anyone paid me the compliment of ransacking my apartment?

I tried tangential thinking, a technique which sometimes
works for me. In this case, that would consist of thinking about
the kind of spaces which had been searched, instead of concentrating on the precise object that might have been stolen. For
instance, a very small drawer in my bedside table had been
opened. I knew that because a paper wedge which I used to
keep that drawer closed had been lying under the bed when I
returned from Mont Sainte-Odile. The drawer itself was

drooping in a way that offended my sense of symmetry. If that drawer had been opened, the coveted object must have been fairly small – a book, perhaps, or a travelling clock, or even a packet of aspirins. So, I could safely conclude that the thief had not come for the coal scuttle or the grand piano – if I had happened to possess either of those items. I was narrowing the field down, and that is always helpful.

I knew, too, that my mattress had been disturbed because of the clumsy way – as I would see it – that the bottom sheet had been replaced. So, what would fit in the space under a mattress? Something flat, obviously. I was within an ace of it now: I knew that. But it took me another day and a half before the answer floated to the surface of my conscious mind – Eoin's photographs!

I had handed those photographs over to the police myself. I suppose that this is why I did not think of them spontaneously as something that should still be in my room. But nobody else knew what I had done with the photographs, except Marianne. What if the person who had sent me the photographs in the first place had decided to take them back again? Or what if the person who had thrown those photos into the fire had discovered that somebody else had fished them out and sent them to me? He might be very keen to have those photographs back. In fact, he might stop at nothing to achieve that objective.

According to the police theory, the person who had thrown those photographs into the fire was probably the same person who had murdered Eoin, and then taken the camera off his dead body. What if that same person had already come calling to my apartment during the previous week, hunting for those photographs? And what if he continued to have ready access to my apartment, day or night? I was now certain that I could not trust the Blum woman as far as I could throw her. Well, where did that leave me? It is not easy to be brave when confronted in the middle of the night by a murderer, in one's pyjamas and bare feet. I admit it: I was scared.

From that day onwards, I began to turn the key in the door whenever I was in the room – day or night. Fortunately, the lock was one of these old-fashioned contraptions where you could turn the key from inside, and give it a half-turn again, so jamming up the key hole to prevent any other key from being inserted in the lock from the outside. That made me feel much safer, and also quite clever.

I went to the Préfecture de Police after the weekend, and asked to be put through to Inspector Péron. I explained to the Inspector what had happened, and my theories about who was responsible. I could hear him thinking on the phone – kissing sounds and oral farts, very French.

'It is a long shot,' he said, 'but you may be right.'

He went on to make an interesting point that I had not thought of: that whoever threw those photos into the fire almost certainly did not know what condition they were in when they were fished out again.

'That means that he does not know that the registration number of his car has, in fact, been obliterated by the flames. He may feel, therefore, that you have him at your mercy. Yes, he may be very anxious to talk to you.'

'Am I meant to find that reassuring?' I asked sarcastically.

There were more kissing and farting sounds, which I endured. I was feeling a need for police protection. The Inspector said: 'No, but, psychologically, this is a most intriguing hand to play. I congratulate you.'

'What on earth are you congratulating me for?' I asked, my

alarm nudging towards panic. 'I am not going to play any bloody "intriguing hand" for you. Forget it. I don't want to end up in the morgue like my poor friend.'

The Inspector changed the subject.

'We have a suspect, you know?'

'Like the last one?' I inquired sceptically, 'The whoremaster of Perpignan – or wherever he was from. Who is this one?'

'He is grey-haired – as we expected – in his middle fifties, and the proud owner of a big black Renault.'

'So, why did he do it?' I asked, unable to conceal my willingness to be convinced.

'He is a suspect. We don't know why he did it, or even *if* he did it.'

'Well, why is he a suspect?'

'Perhaps because he is grey-haired, and has a big black Renault – and also, because his wife died recently in suspicious circumstances.'

That left me perplexed. 'I don't quite see . . . '

'But yes! If our suspect threw the photographs into the fire, and if his wife pulled them out again, and sent them to you, and if he discovered this, and if his wife then dies in suspicious circumstances . . . '

'That's a lot of "ifs". Do you mean that he actually killed her?'

'Maybe. It looked like suicide – an overdose – except, the neighbours say, she was not the suicidal type.'

'But why would he kill her – to punish her for having sent the photographs to me? That sounds like a bit of an over-reaction.'

'Maybe, but what is even more likely is that he killed her to shut her up. Let's suppose she knew that her husband had killed

Eoin. She probably also knew why. By sending you the photo-graphs, she was almost telling you. If you – or we – were to ask her now at point-blank range, she might find the thought of telling us irresistible.

But I'll say no more over the telephone. We are currently investigating our suspect's past. We'll be in touch with you, sooner rather than later.'

'Does he know he is a suspect?' I asked.

'How could he? We have made no overt move in his direc-tion – apart, of course, from condolences from the appropriate police branch of our operations on the death of his dear wife, to put him off the scent.'

'That is really sly!' I exclaimed.

'Yes, isn't it? the Inspector answered. He added. 'I believe that the police force in your country is called "the Civil Guards". Well, we are very civil people too, when it suits us.'

He rang off. I was left wondering whether he should have said that the police force in Ireland was called the civil guards, or the 'civic' guards. I was not sure myself.

CHAPTER FOURTEEN

Two nights later, I had eaten either supper or dinner in the student restaurant, on the Esplanade. It was my main meal of the day, whatever you call that. Nobody in the calorie-coop seemed to be in good spirits or on for a chat, and still less up for a manly game of ping-pong after the meal. Just shovel in the ingredients, and get the hell out of there as fast as you can, seemed to be the order of the day. Outside was equally cheerless – a cold dark night with petulant squalls of rain-sodden wind, that slapped you in the face whichever way you were pointing. I was anxious to get back to my apartment, which, in spite of the chilling effect of bleak Madame Blum, was quite snug.

As I trudged along quickly, shoulders hunched against the elements, I congratulated myself yet again on my sheer ingenuity in making my little pad, not only snug, but also secure from midnight invasion by Blum's unsavoury associates, thanks to the simple expedient of blocking the keyhole with a pre-emptive key.

This was, in truth, a slender basis for security, and my self-satisfied complacency soon slithered back into stale obsession, with familiar and less comfortable preoccupations. For the ten-thousandth time, I asked myself who could have killed Eoin, and why they had done it. As time went on, I was beginning to believe that Eoin had been killed simply because he was so good, and because his murderer was so evil: as simple as that – a light-and-darkness thing. Why did Cain kill Abel? That, after all, is the prototype murder – the paradigm killing of human history. During my 'retreat' at Mont Saint-Odile, I had stumbled on St John the Evangelist's take on that Cain and Abel story. He writes in his first letter, 'Cain cut his brother's throat simply because his own life was evil, and his brother lived a good life.' Is that the heart-breaking truth? Is that the solution to every murder mystery? Is that why Eoin had to die? Perhaps intuitively I had known it from the beginning, from that very first night.

Now, at last, when we were probably on the point of knowing the answers to all our questions – it seemed likely that Inspector Péron was closing in on the murderer – I had to ask myself another more personal, and less comfortable, series of questions. When I knew at last who this person was – this murderer, this grey-haired driver of a luxury car – would I really hate him? Would I want him to die? Would I even be prepared to kill him myself? I was gung-ho for answering all of those questions with a thundering 'YES', until I came to an abrupt halt, with the disturbing realisation that Eoin himself would almost certainly want to forgive his murderer. Like Jesus, and St Stephen, and so many other losers. That stopped me in my tracks. I stood still there on the sidewalk, speechless, opening and closing my mouth like a goldfish in a bowl. When coherent articulation returned to me, I exhaled a raucous protest, 'For Christ's sake, Eoin, will you be reasonable!'

I knew in my heart that he would not be reasonable. Meanwhile, a woman who had been approaching on the same pavement as myself hastily crossed to the other side of the road.

I had arrived on the v-shaped promontory formed by two converging streets, on which St Maurice's church is built. I was idly wondering whether he was the renowned black St Maurice, who had been such a fearless crusader. That would be an unusual choice of patron for one of the more well-heeled districts in Strasbourg, where black mightn't be regarded as beautiful.

A grey van was parked by the side of the church. Two burly men stood behind it. One of the men was opening the back of the van, as if they were making an evening delivery. The other chap stepped back to allow me to pass behind the van, as my road home lay in that direction. At this moment, the fellow who had been opening the van suddenly addressed me, asking me if I were Monsieur Andrew Olden. The pronunciation of both my first and second name was only approximate, but I was used to that, having lived in France before English became one of the vernaculars of the European movement. I recognised my name easily enough, but was totally surprised. Could it be that there was something in that van that could be of interest to me? I acknowledged my name, and was going on to respond with 'Why?', but I never got that far.

A split-second too late I recognised my mistake. I had stepped, unsuspecting, between a pair of heavyweights, who must have seen me as easy meat. From the meat's point of view, it was like being caught between the claws of a gigantic forceps, lifting me up, right off my feet, by the shoulders and the seat of my pants, then flinging me, face-forward, into the back of the van. One of the gorillas leaped after me, sat on my rump, and manacled my hands behind my back. Meanwhile, the guy standing at the back of the van roughly tied my lower legs together with a rope. Within seconds, it seemed, I was lying on my face, on the filthy floor of the van, unable to move hand or foot. The captor who had followed me into the van stayed sitting beside me on the floor. The other guy slammed the back doors of the van, went round to the front, and started driving. It had all happened so suddenly, so quickly, and so violently, that I had not had the reflex to defend myself, or even to cry for help.

The van was gathering speed before I began to shout. As if on cue for this moment, my minder instantly planted his fat ass on my back, crushing my arms, and making the coarse ropes that tied them bite cruelly into my wrists. Lying on your face and rib-cage, on a hard floor in a closed van, with eighteen stones of bully beef sitting on your back, it's simply not possible to get up a shout that will be heard above the din of an engine with rattling cylinders. Shouting was not an option. Neither, I quickly realised, was breathing – which was much more frightening. Soon I was gasping and sobbing to get a little air into my lungs. Fat Ass, as I christened him in this moment of terror, was strangling me as surely as if his two hands were clasped around my throat. It was agony. I panicked. I pleaded, croaking and whinging. I passed out.

When I revived, Fat Ass had resumed his position beside me. He had taught me, in this sudden and sickening episode, who was boss. I realised, too, that this animal was probably an experienced torturer, and that torturers know all the secrets of anatomy – what it is capable of, and how to hurt it. What shocked and frightened me most, was how casually and quickly he had been able to scare the living lights out of me. I am certain that there was nothing haphazard about what he did to me.

It was a deliberate and grim warning: 'You are totally in my power. I can do anything to you, and go anywhere in you, even to the most secret and sacred places.'

I understood something of the degradation and the terror that a girl – or indeed a boy – experiences at the hands of a rapist. Rape, as I have since learned, is widely used in warfare. It is not about sex, nor even about a twisted thirst for pleasure. Rape is about violence, subjection, and humiliation. I became very afraid of this man. He was evil, and he was cruel.

My captors had spoken in French. I could not identify any particular regional accent. Age? Both of them in their mid to late forties, and both strong, tough bully-boys that, I guessed that they were, or had been, soldiers. The operation of my capture had been carried out with such military precision.

Our journey lasted about an hour. By the time I had got over the shock and trauma of being pitched on my face into a van, and practically strangled when I started to shout, I had lost or missed all sense of the direction in which we were travelling. I set myself to assess my situation as calmly as I could. Who the hell would want to kidnap me – a graduate student on a scholarship? I had little doubt that it had nothing to do with my fabulous wealth or my exotic good looks. I knew it must concern Eoin's photographs, and, ultimately, his murderer.

Neither of my two assailants was particularly middle-aged or grey-haired. Clearly, they were only the messenger boys. How had they recognised me? I felt sure that it was that bitch Blum, who had let the ransacker into my room a few nights before, who had now also given those two cut-throats an accurate description of my looks and apparel, together with my habitual movements and itineraries. It was probably she, too, who had suggested to them the *presqu'île* on which St Maurice's church was built as a suitably isolated place to drag me into their van on my way back from the Esplanade. I realised, too late, that I had allowed her to know much more about me than was I should have.

I subsequently found out that I was not wholly correct about how my captors had recognised me. They were, in fact, already in possession of my library card for the Bibliothèque Nationale, which carried my photograph. I had not missed it off my desk when I came back from Mont Sainte-Odile, but this meant that whoever had ransacked my room had not come away completely empty-handed. These two thugs knew what I looked like, even if Blum had not given them a description of my person.

During the last quarter of our journey we were steadily climbing. I guessed then that we had been travelling south-west from Strasbourg, into the Vosges mountains. We pulled up at a pleasant farmhouse, which had been converted tastefully into what was a *residence sécondaire* for some lucky bourgeois from Strasbourg, anxious to escape the summer heat. I could see, even in the dark, that the original homestead had had a second storey added to it. The building was splendidly situated on a spur of the mountain, commanding a magnificent vista, while being itself quite isolated. No point shouting here either, I told myself ruefully, as I was hustled into the house. They had already untied my legs as I lay in the back of the van, so that I could walk inside. Once the door was closed behind us, they also unbound my hands.

This was an enormous relief. With my arms pinioned behind my back, I had been lying on my face, which was bruised and cut from the jolting and lurching of the journey. I had felt every gear-change, every acceleration, every braking, and there had been nothing subtle about our driver's performance. The muscles in my arms, too, were beginning to scream with agonising cramps. I was on – and past – the verge of crying with pain and fright. My morale was as low as it ever gets.

As soon as they had me inside, Fat Ass delivered a little speech that served to bring me down a few notches. He told me I had been brought to this place in order to answer some questions. He advised me – strongly – to answer those questions fully and immediately. Otherwise, he assured me, the consequences would be '*très penibles*' – very painful. I understood clearly that he was talking literally, not metaphorically, if only because metaphors would be a bridge too far for either of those fat oafs.

I asked when I could expect to be questioned. To my surprise, he actually answered me, 'Tomorrow or the next day,' he said, adding helpfully, 'when another person arrives.'

'What other person?' I probed quickly, but that is as much as I was getting. He continued on another tack.

'You will be locked into your room, where you will have every comfort, including a bathroom.' Fat Ass clearly regarded a bathroom as bordering on the exotic. 'The windows are alarmed,' he continued. 'I warn you, do not attempt to open those windows, still less to escape. If you do, you will be severely punished. We have been given instructions to kill you if that is necessary.'

'Whose instructions?' I asked, not expecting an answer; and, of course, I did not get one.

They took me up to my room and locked me in. It was, as the thug had said, a comfortable room. The bed was not made up. Neither was there any heating in the house. But there were several blankets, and what we would now call a duvet on the bed. I would be warm.

The bathroom was clean, and had all the standard fittings, but no hot water in the tap. There was soap. I washed my hands, my face, and eventually my hair and my whole head in cold water. I was dirty, and stank from the floor of that filthy van. I was afraid that any of my cuts or bruises could turn septic if I did not clean them as well as I could. But I was shaking with cold, shock, and fear. Though I would have loved to, I could not face stripping off for a cold shower. There was a nasty bump over my left eye, and a cut which would probably need to be stitched as soon as the swelling had subsided – provided that I was going to live that long.

I climbed into bed fully dressed, covered myself with blankets, and got warm. To my surprise I fell asleep almost immediately, and slept soundly until five o'clock the next morning. When I woke up, I lay in bed and worried. I tried to piece together the fragments of information that I already possessed. Somebody was coming to question me – about the photographs, I did not doubt. Who was that somebody? He was the person who had given instructions that I was to be severely punished – even killed – if I tried to escape, the person who could make it *très penible* for me if I failed to answer his questions. When I began shouting in the van, I had been given an intentional sample of just what '*très penible*' could mean. I most especially did not want that fat stooge suffocating me.

Who were these people? I guessed it must be comprised of those two cut-throats, Blum – I was convinced now that she was one of them – and the big boss, from whom they took their long-distance orders. Alsace, for God's sake, is not exactly beside where *Dépêche du Midi* circulates. But it was in that region that Eoin had been murdered, and it was in that newspaper that somebody had got a version of my name, and an approximate address for me.

It was 'tomorrow or the next day' that the big boss was coming to deal with me. That figured. Eoin's murderer was travelling up from *Dépêche-du-Midi*-land to question, torture, and, very possibly, kill me. Even if I told him all I knew, he would still kill me because, although I had no idea what the hell this thing was all about, I already knew far too much. Eoin was killed because he would recognise this grey-haired man again. I was about to have the fatal pleasure of meeting that same person.

I expected him at every moment the next day, but, by nightfall, he had still not come. I was not allowed out of my room, which, though cold, was beginning to be unpleasantly stuffy: I could not open a window. One or other of the two stooges brought me something to eat three times that day. The food was not bad, and quite plentiful, though I had not much appetite, given my current circumstances. My minders did not answer questions. The one who had been outside the van – whom I was calling, in my mind, Oaf No. Two – was quite genial, inquiring if I had slept well in the morning and suggesting that it was a nice day at lunchtime. I had Fat Ass at supper. He looked at me sourly and said nothing. I was really beginning to detest this individual. I remember thinking at the time, with surprising vehemence – because I'm not an especially bad-tempered or vindictive person, nor one given to crude language – that this fat bastard was bringing me food, and probably, at the same time, working up an appetite to chew my balls off the next time he got a chance.

I spent a long time that day looking out the window. We were high in the Vosges, and the view was truly stunning.

Looking at the crystal white of the snow, the vivid green – almost black – of the plantation conifers, the sparkling blue of the sky, I felt that I was really seeing colours for the first time, and perhaps for the last time, too. I was acutely conscious that I was in deep, deep trouble.

As I gazed through the window, I had a strange feeling that I had been in this place before, or perhaps that I was viewing a panorama that I had previously seen from a different vantage point, maybe from an opposite ridge of the mountains. In the distance and from this height, I could see that down in the valley – though the valley itself was at a considerable height – there was some sort of installation, a military camp perhaps, or one of those scientific research stations. There seemed to be long lines of low buildings; huts. Strangely, there did not seem to be anybody around. No sign of smoke came from the chimneys, and no vehicles were parked outside any of the units. What could it be?

I went to bed early to keep warm; the night was viciously cold. I was also very tired. There is nothing so exhausting as to be staring torture and death in the face, and to have nothing else to do but to wait, to worry, and to be very afraid. Mercifully, I fell asleep almost immediately. But as I slept, something in me must have remained alert, vigilant, and anxiously searching. On the stroke of three o'clock the next morning, I was suddenly wide awake with a convulsive jolt. Already stumbling out of the bed, I found myself running to the window. The night was dark, but down in the valley, there were tiny points of light, as if all along an airport runway seen from high in the sky. They outlined the long narrow buildings that I had seen the previous day. 'Yes,' I said, barely whispering. 'YES!' I shouted recklessly, not caring who heard me. ' Natzweiler-Struthof!' In one leap of the mind I had understood everything. It was as if a deadly snake had struck again and again, suffusing my heart in a flood of toxic emotions – shock, fear, anger, deep sadness, and an almost overwhelming sense of menace. In that moment I didn't know whether I was going to faint or die.

Instead, I staggered back into bed. That, I know, must seem like a ridiculous anti-climax – low comedy, indeed, in the context of what was just about to become a heroic narrative. But comedy, or at least the absurd, is the other face of tragedy. And, anyhow, what other options did I have – except to keep warm and to do some hard and urgent thinking?

It was not yet strictly logical in my mind, more a question of convergences. But from that moment on, everything that had puzzled me about Eoin's death was rapidly coming into focus. My mind had taken an enormous leap, and I knew that I was right. After long months of painful bewilderment, at last I knew who had killed my friend, and for what reason.

I now knew, too, who or what I was up against. For Eoin's sake, for the sake of a multitude of innocent victims, and for the sake of my own skin – to which I am ardently devoted, indeed literally attached – the non-hero that I had always presumed I was had been transformed into a gutsy street fighter. Back against the wall, I was determined to fight, to survive, and to win. At very least, I would go down fighting. I knew, too, that there would be no quarter given, no Queensbury Rules, no Geneva Convention, no fair play in this struggle. I was fully committed to using fair means or foul, to play clean, or to play as dirty as it gets.

Natzweiler-Struthof was the only concentration camp established by the German Reich on French territory. Of course, from the German point of view, it was not on French territory at all, because Alsace and Lorraine had been annexed once again as part of the German Reich. I had visited the camp shortly after arriving in Strasbourg in October 1967, and again with a group of students in April 1968, less than a year before my present story began. Natzweiler-Struthof had both fascinated and horrified me. The camp was in operation between May 1941 and the beginning of September 1944. It is estimated that as many as fifty thousand prisoners were interned there over the three years of its active existence. They came from various countries: France and Germany, Belgium, Poland and Russia, Holland, and Norway. They were mostly members of resistance movements in their countries of origin. They were to be destroyed by forced labour, and to disappear without their families ever knowing where and when – or even if – they had died. Some were Jews, Gypsies, communists, and male homosexuals, though most of these – especially the Jews – were transported or force-marched east, to mass extermination camps.

In autumn 1944, as Allied troops drew close to the camp, 141 French Resistance fighters were murdered at Struthof. The next day, the remaining population of the camp was evacuated to Dachau. Hundreds – perhaps as many as a thousand – perished on that death march. On 23 November 1944, when the French army finally entered the camp, they found it deserted.

Struthof was not an extermination camp, but there were many executions. As many as half of those imprisoned there died from forced labour, starvation, and brutal treatment by SS guards. There were also sinister medical experiments, and a steady supply of corpses and body parts for the medical school in Strasbourg University. No questions asked, you may be sure, about the nationality, politics, or religion of the organ donors, or even of those whose 'spontaneous generosity' extended so far as their whole cadavers. I had known this much about the camp from my former visits. I was about to learn a lot more of its tragic and sordid history.

As I write, there is an imposing monument to the Departed at Struthof, which I don't think was in place in 1968. It is so high that I would surely have seen it from any angle, and recognised where I was from the very first moment of my incarceration. There used also to be a small camp museum recording the sufferings and the shame of Stuthof. Nazi supporters – still in vindictive and contemptuous denial of the facts of history even thirty years after the war – succeeded in burning down this silent but eloquent testimony in May 1976.

CHAPTER FIFTEEN

He arrived at midday the following day, driving a medium-sized blue Citroën, not a large black Renault. Aged in his mid to late fifties, he was tall and athletic-looking, and did indeed have plenty of grey hair. My two jailers were already outside to greet him, standing stiffly to attention. Incredibly, they were both wearing swastika arm-bands – and so was he as he got out of his car. They exchanged a Nazi salute, probably gurgling 'Heil Hitler', even though that particular poison dwarf had been incinerated a quarter of a century previously. To be honest, I do not know what they gurgled, because I was watching the absurd comedy from behind a closed window upstairs. It was like a bad war film, one of those where all the German officers are icily polite, and go around the place saying 'very in-ter-est-ing' with superbly sinister suavity. It was the purest make-believe, a children's game. Yet that game had killed Eoin, and probably this man's own wife, and it was now bidding fair to dispose of me for good measure – if I did not play my cards very well indeed.

One good result of our distinguished visitor's arrival was

that twenty minutes later the radiators started to groan and creak. The heat was coming on. That was welcome – I had been very cold. And there was hot water in the tap, too. Before long, I could at last have the luxury of a shower. My lunch was delivered in the usual way by Fat Ass. I never, until it ceased to matter, get to know either of their names. Lunch was more elaborate than on the previous day, and there was even a glass of wine. This, I supposed, reflected either fallout from the feast prepared for the big chief, or a condemned man's last supper. I would not demean myself by asking Fat Ass when I could expect the Führer to be dropping in. The great man was obviously in no hurry, enjoying his own meal, and, at the same time, twisting the screw even tighter on my pit-of-the-stomach dread. I drank the wine, wishing that I had at least two more glasses to go with it. I must have done wee-wee about four times in the next hour, which is just how anxiety takes me.

What should my strategy be? I had asked myself that same question hundreds of times over the last thirty-six hours. The immediate priority was to save my own skin. I was crystal clear on that point. I also knew that, in order to achieve that objective, I would have to lie through my teeth. My only fear was that the lies would not be big enough or good enough. I further knew that, like an old rat caught in a trap, I would probably have to gnaw off my own foot in order to escape. This meant that I would have to seem to disown my lifelong friend, Eoin, and conceal my anger – my utter revulsion – in the presence of his murderer. If I was to have any hope of getting out of this house alive, Eoin's killer must not suspect that I was bullshitting him up to the eyeballs; he must actually believe me. So, what would my story be?

I could tell him, for instance, that I had never received the photographs at all. Neat, but too risky. Madame Blum – once again, I was convinced that she was one of them – could have told the murderer that I had received a packet a short time ago. I could only hope that she had not eavesdropped on my telephone conversation with Péron telling him about the photographs. That conversation, of course, had to be in French. She also had the entrée to my room, which she was meant to clean. Her activities in that connection were less than zealous, but I already suspected her of snooping. There had been a curious incident about my underwear, too embarrassing to even think about. I earnestly hope that, at least, she did not try it on. But her access to my room was yet another way that Blum could have confirmed that I had received the photos. They were lying on my desk overnight and into the following afternoon before I'd had a chance to deliver them to the police.

Alternatively, I could actually tell the murderer the truth: that I had received the photos and had given them to the police, but that the registration number of his car had been obliterated by the flames, so that there was nothing that the police could do about it. That, I was sure, would be tantamount to signing my own death warrant. Having diligently reported to the police once when I was handing over the photos, I would certainly do so again, now that I could recognise Eoin's killer – even if I did not know his name. At this stage his name did not matter. I could describe him and his two companions in detail, give the location of the house at Struthof, which would be awash with fingerprints, and report other tell-tale traces of the trio. I could even give the police the registration number of the blue Citroën in which the guy had arrived in the Vosges, together with detailed descriptions of the Nazi posturing of these absurd and highly dangerous fanatics.

The plain fact was that, once the photographs had not been

found in my room, Eoin's murderer had almost certainly concluded that I had given them to the police. I had been captured, now, for the purpose of being interrogated – specifically about the condition of the fire-damaged photo of the black Renault. I would then be killed, and my body would never be found. There was no way that this murderer would ever let me walk free knowing the things about him that I had learnt over the last few days, and would inevitably continue to learn now that I was about to meet him face to face. I reflected that this latter-day Nazi zealot was probably the same guy as Inspector Péron was closing in on even now. Could that make a difference? Could I fling it in his face? 'Hey, Fritz, or Hans, or whatever the hell you call yourself – you don't seem to realise that your little game is up. The *flics* already know that you murdered Eoin because you were afraid that he was going to denounce you for some of the shit that you did during the war – probably right here in Struthof. They already know that you murdered your own wife because she sent me the photographs – including a fine shot of your big black Renault. They're just waiting to fill in some more details from your dirty past before they haul you in. And if I were to disappear now – which I already have, two or three days ago – the police will know exactly whose door to come knocking at. So, like a good fellow, why not do yourself a favour by giving yourself up quietly now? At least I could say, in mitigation, that you had not roughed me up in captivity, that you had turned on the hot water and the heating, and that you had even given me a glass of quite drinkable wine for my lunch. Look on the bright side: you could easily be out in thirty years' time, unless the shit that you did during war was really too disgusting, and they decide to hang you. Well, you win some, and you lose some. Okay?'

This was, I had to admit, the most futile of wishful thinking.

Even without seeing my adversary face to face, I knew that he was entirely ruthless. He was not the kind to give up until he was entirely checkmated and cornered. Even then, he would very probably take his suicide pill rather than be captured alive. By that point, I would be long dead and fed to the fishes.

Besides, there were too many uncertainties. I did not know for sure if the guy realised that I had given the photos to the police. I did not know whether he knew that the photograph of his car had been so damaged by fire as to make the registration number illegible. Finally, I did not know whether this was the same man that Péron was pursuing, and, even if it was, whether that line of inquiry might still prove to be a complete red herring. My main problem was that, although very willing to lie through my teeth, I did not know precisely which lies to tell.

What I *did* know was that this man had decided to take me captive, and, therefore, to inevitably reveal to me all sorts of things about himself and his companions. The high probability was that he now intended to question me, to torture me if necessary, and, having found out what he wanted to know, to kill me. If he did not kill me, I would have no end of motivations to lead the police straight to him at the first opportunity.

All roads led to the same conclusion: my only road out of a very tight corner was to lie as I had never lied before – big, cunning lies. It was literally a question of life or death; of *my* life or *my* death. I did not feel the slightest twinge of guilt about lying to this thug. I was fighting for my life, and to see Eoin avenged. Besides, in my book, nobody – but nobody – had any right whatsoever to the truth, if the truth would make him still more determined to torture and kill me.

I knew that, theoretically at least, wisdom, knowledge, discernment, and agile footwork are vaguely the Holy Spirit's department. That is what we had been taught in school. So, although it felt strange, I prayed to the Holy Spirit to help me to tell some really whopping lies. Actually – because the killer pushed open the door quite suddenly and came in – I had only time for a brief 'ejaculation' – a word that, incredibly, has a pious as well as a sexual meaning. In the spiritual sense, it means a quick and fervent prayer. The word had caused so much ribald sniggering in school, where it had been used frequently by a particularly sanctimonious teacher, that I could never forget it. Now, in my hour of desperate need, I did remember to emit a heartfelt and strictly spiritual ejaculation. Such are the by-product benefits of a good Catholic education.

So, he came in. A man as I have described him earlier: middle-aged, but strong and tall. A hard face. He would have been well capable of snapping Eoin's neck, and of carrying his lifeless body a short distance. As he approached me, I got a vaguely familiar chemical whiff, which I identified as the same unpleasant musk that I had detected in my room when I got back from Mont Sainte-Odile. So, it was this same guy who had probably searched my room for the photographs. I figured that I sure-as-hell knew the agenda for our upcoming conversations.

Another thing I quickly realised was that this man was more than a little drunk. My advantage, I thought again – as if we were having a jolly game of tennis.

The Holy Spirit, as well as being a source of good ideas, is also in charge of fortitude and daring. Amazingly, from piss-afraid, as I had been for the last two days, I now felt suddenly calm and strong – and that the Spirit was really giving me excellent value for my solitary ejaculation. Next thing was – I did not stand up. Body language is important. I sensed that by remaining seated, I had actually disconcerted him. Good. Then, before he could say anything, I grabbed the high ground.

'Thank you for sending me those photographs,' I exclaimed, in an even voice that surprised and excited me. Before he could say that he had not sent them to me, I added, without quite knowing what I meant: 'That may have changed everything.'

Where was this crazy talk leading me? I simply did not know. I was suddenly high – almost manic – as if it were I who'd had that feed of drink for lunch.

'What do you mean?' he said curtly, but uncertainly. I could see him wondering if it could perhaps work to his advantage to pretend that he *had* sent me the photographs. He sat down, a little too heavily. Good.

'Listen,' I heard myself saying, 'I was genuinely touched by what you did there. You were taking a terrible risk – I could have gone to the police . . . '

'You mean you did not go to the police?' he asked incredulously.

I spat. I actually *spat*! I cannot remember having ever spat indoors, before or since, except, of course, into a washbasin or the lavatory.

'The police? No way!' I exclaimed, and spat again. 'I admit that I was going to give the photos to the police – until I found out that the brainless idiots think that *I* did it, that *I* murdered Eoin. They say that Eoin and I were little friends – they mean lovers – who had had a lovers' quarrel. Of course, they despise that sort of thing from a height. Unfortunately, I had given them some grounds for their suspicions. You see, I had been visiting Fontevraud the same day. That is very near the place where they say that Eoin was killed. So, they were able to fix me more or less at the scene of the crime. Anyhow, I don't think the police are going to waste too much time on what they regard as a pair of foreign queers.' The French word I used was '*pédés*', which is equivalently contemptuous. I added, 'I don't think you need worry too much.'

I continued. 'Besides, if you want to know, I did not give the photographs to the police, because I figured that they would not believe me about some mysterious fairy godmother sending them to me in the post. They would much prefer to believe that I had stolen Eoin's camera off his body, and invented a whole cock-and-bull story as to how I had received the photographs in the post, from some anonymous well-wisher. In fact, that would have made them even more suspicious of me, instead of less. They would think that I was just trying to muddy the waters, and let myself off the hook.'

He looked at me with something approaching interest, and said, almost wonderingly, 'This is not at all what I expected.' He added, as an after-thought, 'Were you lovers?'

'What do you think?' I replied, donning my best poker player face.

He did not answer. Instead he said, 'Eoin, is that how you pronounce his name? It is a nice name, and he was a nice boy. Unfortunately, I told him far too much – about myself. I think he reminded me of dreams I had in my youth, of what I might have become, if the world were a very different place. But there is a war on; I had no choice but to neutralise your friend, when he took that photograph of my car. I saw him doing it in my rear mirror when he got out of the car.'

'There is a war on?' I asked. It was my turn to act incredulous. So I did.

'Oh yes,' he insisted, 'between the Reich and the dregs of society, degenerate sub-humans. I mean communists, gypsies, half-wits and, above all, Jews. We, the master-race, have never surrendered. We are still working and fighting to save civilisation from the chaos into which it is rapidly sinking. This so-called Student Revolution, for instance – inexcusable and intolerable! But it is only one example of total disorder.' The word he used was '*pagaille*'. I could not help thinking of Eoin's arrogant bishop, with his talk of insubordination and *effronterie*.

I noticed that this fellow had not listed homosexuals amongst the usual Nazi catalogue of hate-figures, and 'degenerate sub-humans'. On the assumption that he believed that Eoin and I had been lovers, this discreet silence probably indicated a willingness to ingratiate himself with me, an eagerness to do business? After all, he *did* want something that I apparently had. He needed those photographs. He was most likely trying to work out what combination of stick and carrot would be most effective to induce me to hand them over.

Even as we spoke, I had no doubt that if he did ever succeed in getting his hands on what he wanted, he would murder me at the earliest opportunity, as both a fool and a knave who knew far too much. This man is highly intelligent, I said to myself; he is also entirely ruthless. He is a bit drunk just at the moment, but he will be sober again tomorrow. So, is there any area or aspect of his personality where he is habitually weak, unintelligent, or – as it were – permanently inebriated? Any Achilles heel where I could have a serious chance of deceiving him? If there is, I told myself, that is exactly where I have to concentrate the entire fire-power of my sustained mendacity. The answer came to me.

Even I am diffident about the claim that the Holy Spirit was my accomplice in a dedicated campaign of lying. So, let me repeat as a pragmatic fact – and without implicating anyone – divine, angelic, human, or even demonic, that the answer came to me. It was that this man's deranged obsession with the whole Nazi worldview proved that, in that respect, he was a blithering idiot. In that context, and on that subject, he was as gullible and naive as a child. He had already believed lies that are as crass and as crude as anything I could ever hope to sell him. So, I told myself, you have got to shoot point-blank at the bull's eye of this guy's demented Nazi bullshit. *Heave-ho!* I went to it with a heart and a half.

'My heart leapt,' I lied ferociously, 'when I saw you from my window, giving the Nazi salute. I have been sickened by the vast disorders of the squalid student rebellion. I have the misfortune to be a student myself.'

I called it a rebellion, not a revolution – which is what the students called it.

'The students have allowed themselves to be led by the nose, by communists, anarchists, and by other such sub-human degenerates.'

He was watching me closely, wondering, no doubt, whether I was serious and sincere, or whether I was selling him a load of manure. People who have no sense of humour themselves find it very difficult to tell when somebody else – and perhaps especially an Irishman – is giving them the blarney treatment.

'De Gaulle has been one of the great disappointments of my life,' I continued. 'I thought he was a leader, but leaders need to know how to be ruthless at times. Only fascism can save France, and, now, civilisation. The troubles caused by the student rabble have died down for the present, but just wait and see – they'll be back worse than ever within a few months. International Communism and the new Jewish Order will see to that. We absolutely need a true Führer.'

I was appalled at the facility with which I was talking such grotesque nonsense, and passing it off effortlessly as what I really thought myself. It was laughable that anyone could swallow such complete drivel. Perhaps that is exactly why fanatics are so very dangerous: they *do* believe the most shocking lies; their whole lives revolve around them. I ploughed on.

'Listen, sir – I am sorry, I don't know your name . . .'

He hesitated, then said, 'My name is Commandant Josef Schmitt of the Waffen SS, the Führer's personal elite. That is not my real name, of course, I acquired it from a traitorous member of the French Maquis, an Alsatian – so, a German, and, therefore, a traitor. Well, unfortunately, he went missing.'

He smirked as he said 'unfortunately', and then actually winked conspiratorially.

'That was our way, you know, *Nacht und Nebel*. Nobody ever knew what became of him. But we took care of him all right!'

He sniggered, looked closely at me again, and continued.

'Schmitt ended up here in Struthof. We hanged him because he was a traitor to the Fatherland. That an Alsatian could have French sympathies, we tolerated such abject thinking: but that he should actively plot against the Reich and commit acts of sabotage against our armed forces, that was betrayal, and rightly punishable by death.

So, yes, my name is assumed. It has to be, because of what I was doing during the war.'

He grinned humourlessly, baring his teeth like a bad tempered animal.

'Perhaps I'll tell you about that later,' he continued encouragingly. I said nothing.

'But my rank – Commandant – is genuine,' he added. 'Of course, I cannot use it openly now. That would be impossible in the present loathsome situation.'

As we talked, I was all the time aware that I was walking a

tightrope. Schmitt, who was half-drunk, had really begun to tell me things. He was quite clearly obsessive about the worldview that he, his two oafs, and God knows how many other zealots had created for themselves. Later, tomorrow, when he had sobered up, he could decide that I was really one of them and let me live, at least for as long as it took me to produce those photographs. On the other hand, he could decide that he had already told me far too much – as he had, no doubt, told Eoin far too much – and that he must liquidate me immediately, just as he had Eoin.

I went forward – simply because there was no way I could turn back now. I had already told lies that really hurt me. I told more. It was no longer a battle of wits about whose ideas were the cleverest; it was a fight for survival: *my* survival.

'This Eoin guy, he was Irish too, so I suppose it was inevitable that we should meet up sooner or later. He was OK, but a bit too pious for my liking. I am sad that he had to die, but I accept what you say – that it was warfare. I suppose you could say that he got caught in the cross-fire. You had no choice. I would have done the same.'

That was so awful that I thought I had really overdone it this time, that he *must* see through such sick-making hypocrisy. But I had actually seen the swastika arm-bands and Hitler salutes with my own eyes. This guy was wired to the moon. He was a dangerous lunatic, precisely because he was so chillingly sane and consistent, according to his own skewed perspective on the world. He stood up, and walked over to me. He shook my hand and said, ' "Caught in the cross-fire", that is very well put; that is exactly what happened. You are a very intelligent and unusual young man. It is good to be able to talk to you. We somehow find the courage to endure this long and harsh struggle in almost complete isolation, because we know that, in the long run, victory will be to the strongest and the most ruthless. Willpower is the decisive factor. It is in that context that your friend had to die. I bore him no ill-will, but he made a stupid mistake. Stupid mistakes must not be made in warfare.'

I was about to think up something even more emetic to say in reply to this garbage, but Schmitt suddenly seized me by the arm and exclaimed: 'You must give me those photographs.'

He was staring straight into my eyes, like a cobra hypnotising a rabbit. But I was no rabbit – not any longer. In fact, having thrown all decency to the winds, I was transformed into some kind of a mongoose, the only creature on earth that is not afraid of a cobra. I stared straight back.

'You are very welcome to them,' I replied.

I thought that he would ask immediately where the photographs were – and this would undoubtedly be the crunch. Could he possibly believe the pathetic lie that I had concocted for this moment? A chain is as strong as its weakest link. I had been doing so well with my lies so far that I was thoroughly horrified and ashamed of myself. I had been brought up always to tell the truth. How could I be so effortlessly deceitful? Could it really be all down to the Holy Spirit? Or was the chain of lies about to unravel and disintegrate – revealing what the Holy Spirit really thought of me? And what then?

To my astonishment, instead of pursuing the question of the photographs, the SS Commandant suddenly flung open the door and gestured for me to pass through. 'Let's drink to that,' he exclaimed. I preceded him down the stairs. The two gorillas were waiting for us, and probably astonished to see me, not only alive, but seemingly confident that I would die of old age, in my own bed.

The Commandant addressed them curtly, with two syllables: '*Sortez*' – 'Leave us'. They saluted, and left. He did not ask me what I would like to drink. As a young man, my repertoire was either beer or wine. I certainly never touched spirits. He poured me half a tumbler of neat calvados, and the same for himself. I availed of a brief absence on his part – to see Mrs Murphy about a dog – to empty most of my ration into a potted plant, which I doubt did well in the aftermath. I needed to keep my wits about me for telling high-quality lies. Besides, I could not trust this cut-throat's sudden geniality. I had an uneasy feeling that – just when I thought I was leading him a merry dance – he might be doing exactly the same thing to me, only better. Fire-water might be his version of the lie-detector, and even more effective than torture. And the lies were certainly pouring out of me thick and fast.

Not that the man gave me much opportunity to tell either the truth or untruths for the next two hours. That may have been his original plan. But he was one of those people who the more they drink, the more they monopolise the conversation. In a short time, little more was required of me than encouraging grunts and exclamations. His Nazi thing was totally obsessive and all-embracing. Yet he seemed to have a prodigious need to justify himself, and an insatiable thirst for affirmation and approval. Needless to say, he got both from me – in the form of obsequious horse-shit. Meanwhile he refilled his own glass twice. He replenished my glass once, but I just fiddled with it and he had ceased to notice.

He told me that he had bought the house that we were sitting in six years previously.

'It serves as a retreat during the heat of summer. I have done well in business. Besides, some influential people, who share the same views as myself, have been generous to me.'

He got on to the topic of Simon Wiesenthal, the famous hunter of Nazi war criminals, about whom I had never even heard until that evening. His hatred of Wiesenthal was visceral and virulent.

'He is a Russian savage and Jewboy who opened a Jewish Documentation Centre in Vienna, with the exclusive aim of hunting down German war heroes. He has just published a book called *The Murderers Among Us*, an obscene tissue of libels and defamation. He was also personally responsible for the murder of Adolf Eichmann at the hands of Jewish swine. Eichmann was one of the towering geniuses of social strategy during the first phase of our struggle, which had as its goal the racial purity of our people and, as a logical consequence, the elimination of vermin.'

I had certainly heard of Eichmann. He was the chief of the Gestapo Jewish Department who had masterminded and supervised the 'Final Solution', which – shorn of its uninformative title – was simply the mass murder of millions of Jews and minorities. He disappeared at the end of the war. It was Wiesenthal, I subsequently learnt, who had relentlessly pursued Eichmann, and eventually traced him to Argentina, where he was living under the assumed name of Ricardo Klement. Eichmann was kidnapped by Israeli agents, brought to Israel, tried, and hanged in May 1961.

Schmitt listed off names of other 'war heroes' who had been cornered by Wiesenthal: Karl Silberbauer, Franz Stangl, and Hermine Braunsteiner – who had married an Irish-American called Ryan after the war, and settled down to be a nice house-wife in Queens, New York. But Mrs Ryan had a past. She had supervised the killing of several hundred children at Majdanek.

I barely recognised any of these names in 1968, but phonetically noted down as many as I could remember the next day, and checked on them later. What they all had in common was that they had cooperated in the mass murder of defenceless civilians, many of them mere children, and the great majority of them Jews. If Schmitt was calling these monsters war heroes, he must have been a monster himself, and – as somebody said about Lord Byron – 'mad, bad, and dangerous to know'. I was worried about that last bit. I already knew Schmitt much too well for comfort. There was nothing I could do about it. He had bludgeoned his way into my life, uninvited.

Schmitt boasted then that he had infiltrated the Simon Wiesenthal Centre, and planted persuasive evidence that he himself had been killed in 1956. This, together with the new identity that he had stolen from the *maquisards*, made it safe for him to brazenly occupy this house in the Vosges, overlooking Natzweiler-Struthof, where, he told me complacently, he had spent the happiest, most fulfilling, and most 'creative' years of his whole life.

I was at once horrified and fascinated. He reminded me of the mythical basilisk, whose very breath was said to be fatal. I knew with chilling lucidity that the more things this basilisk breathed to me, the more motives he would have to murder me later, as he had murdered Eoin, presumably for exactly the same reasons. It occurred to me, even as we talked, that this was probably this basilisk's peculiar brand of sadism. He would feed you information until the penny dropped, and you realised with sick horror that he could never afford to release you now, because you knew too much, and that, in fact, you had been digging your own grave just by listening. The basilisk of mythology was said to have been hatched from a cock's egg, by a serpent.

In a grotesque way, that seemed to fit Herr Schmitt admirably.

I plunged compulsively on. 'What did you do at Struthof? I mean, what was your job?'

He smiled sardonically. 'I suppose you think I was a common screw, or perhaps a cook for the pig-swill we ate, eh?'

I made vaguely deprecatory noises, but at this stage of his drunkenness, he was no longer interested in what I was thinking. Instead, he was wholly intent on cudgelling me into craven acceptance of his worldview, and, more specifically, of the unspeakable atrocities that had happened right here, in this very place.

'I was a medical researcher,' he declared proudly, 'at the cutting edge of experimentation.'

I gasped at that, and at his unfortunate, presumably unintended wordplay. He did not notice. It was already common knowledge that in several of the concentration and extermination camps, in the name of medical research, the most hideous experiments had been carried out on people who were regarded as non-persons, scum, the cesspool of humanity. Those horrible 'procedures' were frequently embarked upon without any anaesthetic beforehand, or any antidote or sedation afterwards. The victims were often left to die in agony, without even the consideration of a bullet through the brain to alleviate their torment. I could not restrain myself from blurting out the next question.

'But were you even a doctor?'

He coloured – not with embarrassment but out of sheer vexation.

'What the hell has that got to do with anything? The point is that I had a talent bordering on genius. It was my duty not to squander that priceless gift in cowardly feelings of compassion for criminals and other despicable individuals. My mission was to use my skill to fight disease, and so make life safer, longer, and more pleasant for people who were worthy of my sacrifice.'

I felt my mouth fall open in blank astonishment. I wanted to shout – '*Your* sacrifice, you miserable shit?' Instead I inquired, mildly, 'So what kind of experiments did you do?'

His answer was detailed and utterly disgusting. He talked about poor wretches being lacerated, then having their wounds infected with mustard gas, or having the gas injected into their veins, being forced to drink it in liquid form, or to inhale it.

I knew enough about the camps to realise that this was actually comparatively minor, that it would not rate more than a footnote in the records of torments that thousands of other prisoners endured in the name of 'medical science' in many concentration camps in Central and Eastern Europe. But it was nonetheless very difficult to listen to. What was particularly sickening was that Schmitt, throughout his obscene narrative, noted the heroic virtue of *his* unflinching gaze and steady hand, as he inflicted agony and listened, unmoved, to the piercing screams and cries of his victims.

He continued, brimming with self-importance. 'Of course, my most enduring work was to assist SS-Hauptsturmführer Professor Dr August Hirt in his vital work of assembling a collection of Jewish skeletons, and other sub-human hominoids for the Reich University of Strasbourg.'

I pricked up my ears at the mention of my university. He went on. 'This research was vital to demonstrate clearly the superiority of the Nordic race. Professor Hirt was, as you must know, a very eminent academic and, in fact, the chairman of the Reich University of Strasbourg.'

I had not known this, and I had never even heard of

Professor Hirt. I felt sure, at that first moment when I *did* hear of him, that successive French governments and the City of Strasbourg must have laboured mightily to ensure that I, and others like me, would never get to hear so much as his name. Romantic dreams of my university, as an old and venerable place, where wisdom and truth, beauty and goodness had always been cherished, were going to take a sad battering, I felt sure. It was almost like being told that my own mother was a whore.

'Where did you get the skeletons?' I asked.

'Where did we get the skeletons?' he mimicked. 'We made them ourselves,' he answered provocatively. 'We went to Auschwitz – where there was a wider variety of sub-humans and criminals. We selected 115 men and woman, mostly Jews, but a few Poles and Asians as well, for good measure. All typical of low-grade species. We brought them back here, gassed them, and stripped the meat off them. That's how you make a skeleton, you know.'

He added as a sick after-thought – a grotesque joke – 'Actually, they didn't have too much meat to strip off them. The cuisine at Auschwitz wasn't exactly cordon bleu, you know.'

I had to swallow my vomit. He laughed, and continued in a lighter vein. 'The proof that we medical researchers are people of higher intelligence is that very few of us have been cornered by lickspittles like Wiesenthal. We are far too clever for that. Josef Mengele, the most eminent of us all, is still at liberty. So is Dr Aribert Heim. And so am I – as you may have noticed. In fact, I am in touch with both Heim and Mengele. Heim actual-ly practised openly in Baden-Baden as a gynaecologist after the war, until the early sixties – even though the criminals in Mauthausen had made him famous with the left-handed compliment of calling him "Doctor Death".'

Schmitt found this funny, and laughed harshly again.

'In 1962 Heim had to disappear, as the Jewboys were getting too close for comfort. But he is still enjoying life – on this side of the Atlantic, I may add. Dr Mengele is – shall we say – a bit further away.

Meanwhile others – I mean non-medical personnel – have been less creative, less clever, and, so, less fortunate. Here in Struthof, for instance, they hanged Franz Berg, and poor old Peter Straub – he was our hangman, and a very busy one, too. I suppose they thought that it was poetic justice to hang the hangman on his own gallows, but he was only doing his job. They would have hanged our Commandant, Fritz Hartjenstein, but he out-witted them by dying before they could string him up.'

'What about August Hirt?' I asked.

'He took the honourable way out. He killed himself in 1945. The miserable bastards! They did not even give brave soldiers an honourable death. They hanged them like common crimi-nals. That's victors' justice for you! But never fear. Our day will dawn. Then it will be our turn. We have the names of all these scoundrels – from Churchill and Eisenhower down to their common hangmen and to the least of their lackeys. Not a single one of them will escape.'

It went on for at least two hours, perhaps more. The guy had been drinking since before he came into my room. When we got downstairs he had consumed most of two tumblers of raw calvados before my eyes. Once he got into his stride, I did not have to say very much at all. I was pleasantly surprised. I had fully expected to be in for a grim battle of wits about the pho-tographs, and if I lost that battle, that they would, first, torture the shit out of me to find out where those photos were, and then, when they had discovered that they were already in the hands of the police – which they would find out much sooner than later, because I was certain that I could not stand up to more than three seconds of torture – they would torture me some more, just for the hell of it, then shoot me or break my neck. Just like what had happened to Eoin.

But, instead of that grim scenario which I had so vividly anticipated for several days, an occasional moan of pleasure or grunt of approbation seemed to be all that was required of me – or even permitted. That scewball went on and on with his obscene rant. When I had got beyond the stage of fascination mingled with sheer repugnance for what he was saying, I eventually got plain bored. There is nothing more wearisome – when you are not drinking yourself – than having to watch somebody with no sense of humour getting progressively more pissed under your nose. It is particularly so, when the sole topic of the monologue is how wonderfully clever he and the Führer are, and how contemptible are all Jews, Gypsies, coloured people, homosexuals, communists, disabled folk, the insane – and indeed everybody else except seven foot giants with blonde hair. Of course, with the exception of his dotey little black-haired Führer with the pubic-puss moustache.

Suddenly he was standing over me, bottle at the ready to top up my glass. I had actually nodded off – which is not really a great idea when you are meant to be fighting for your life. Schmitt found my glass disappointingly full. His eyes narrowed. He clearly belonged to the *in vino veritas* school of interrogators, and had hoped that booze would loosen my tongue – as it had certainly loosened his. 'Do you not like it?' he inquired coldly.

'Oh, it's great!' I replied, as nonchalantly as I could. 'But I'm not used to spirits, see! Beer is all we get in Ireland.'

'Yes, well, let's get down to business. Where are these photographs?'

For the first time, there was an unmistakable note of menace in his voice. I realised, too, that, however much he had drunk – and his speech was slightly but noticeably slurred – his mind was fully focussed. This was the crunch. He had chosen the moment with impeccable timing, when I had finally let down my guard. I waffled a bit – though immediately I knew that this was the wrong tactic. The time for hard-ball had come. This guy could leave me for dead – and that was only one of his more humane options.

'Oh, the photographs, is it? That's a long story.'

He put the bottle, which he had been holding in his hand, on a table. Then he slapped me full in the face. 'No more Mister Nice-Guy,' I thought ruefully.

'Get to the bottom line of your long story – fast,' he commanded through clenched teeth, 'or I swear, you'll be sorry that you'd ever been born.'

If I doubted that proposition as a philosopher, as a pragmatist, I fully believed it. Gathering lost momentum as quickly as I could, I told my most brazen lie. On it depended whether I would walk out of this house on my own two legs, or be carried out of it in a body-bag.

'The photographs are safe with my solicitors in Dublin,' I lied.

'What?' he said stupidly, as if I had suddenly started to speak in Chinese. If he had heard what I had said, he seemed to have some difficulty taking it in. His focus might be good – even in his drunken state – but it was nevertheless narrow: 'Get the photos, beat the crap out of the little shit if necessary, but get the photos. End of plan.' But my story was outside the parameters of that fundamentalist strategy. I could almost see him working out in his head whether he would have to go to Dublin and beat the crap out of my solicitor, too. I could bear this as a sorrow not quite my own. Indeed, a good beating could have a welcome tonic effect on my solicitor.

'Listen,' I continued, before he could interject, 'when I first got those photographs, I had not yet worked out that they were from you, and intended as a friendly gesture. I was scared. I wondered whether sending me the photographs was some crazy guy's way of saying, "We got your little pal – and now we are coming to get you too!" I have told you already that the police think we were a pair of faggots. Well, there are plenty of people around who are violently homophobic, and cruel.'

I did not think it was the moment to remind him that the official position of the Nazi Party was ferociously anti-queer. This homophobia of the 'Master Race' was, of course, sheer hypocrisy. Several of the top people in the Nazi world were enthusiastic sporters of the green carnation – under their jerkins, so to speak.

I paused to see how I was doing, but Schmitt said nothing. He was clearly finding it difficult to absorb the idea that the photograph of the backside of his car – that he so desperately needed – was sitting in a solicitor's office in a foreign country. In his drunken state, he could not get his head around that. I hastened to tell more lies – to cordon off a number of other ways that he could try to achieve his objective.

'My solicitors have two further instructions. First of all, they are to hand over the sealed packet – they don't even know what the contents of the packet are – but they are to hand it over only to me, *in person*. So, letters or telephone calls will produce no result whatsoever, even if they are from me. The second instruction is that if anything happens to me, my solicitors are to send the packet, without delay, to the French police. It is to be sent to Inspector Michel Péron in Orléons, who is handling the investigation into Eoin's murder. That should point the Inspector in the right direction, don't you think?' I added unhelpfully, 'The Inspector is really very bright.'

He shouted, 'I don't believe you, *couillon*, and struck me once more. "*Couillon*" is originally a French word for testicles. It has always amazed me throughout language that some people think so poorly of their genitals.

If the insult did not hurt, the slap did. I said, as casually as I could, 'Well, suit yourself, but I would just like to draw your attention to the fact that it has already been three or four days since I've gone missing. Several people are bound to have noticed. So, there is a certain urgency – from your point of view – if you don't mind me saying so. These photographs will very soon be on their way to the French police, if we don't do something about it.' I thought that the 'we' in the last sentence would really annoy him. Good!

I was just about to add that Marianne, my true love, would surely have noticed a void in her life, and that I had told her that if this ever happened, she should telephone the solicitors immediately and get them to send the incriminating packet to Inspector Péron. This would have been a lie too far. I stopped myself just in time (not out of moral scruples: I had no moral scruples as to what I would tell this rabid dog) but I broke out into a cold sweat at the thought that I had nearly involved Marianne with him. He would almost certainly have contacted her straight away. Perhaps he would have posed as a policeman. Depending on what questions he asked her, she could have let slip – trying to help me – that I had passed the photographs to the police, and that the fire had destroyed all trace of the registration number of his car. That much alone would have been enough to earn each of us a bullet in the brain – as people who knew far too much and whom Schmitt no longer needed.

So, still eager to put pressure on him, I considered telling him instead that Madame Blum would miss me, and report my absence to the police. I quickly decided that I should not say that either. He knew, and I knew, whose side Blum was on. Better to leave well alone.

While I was considering my options, Schmitt was marshalling his wits as well.

He asked me straight out. 'Did the registration number of my car survive the fire? There was a fire, you know. Somebody threw those photographs into a fire.'

'I wonder who,' I could not resist saying. He coloured about the gills. 'Well,' I continued, 'somebody must have pulled them out again. One or two of the numbers is illegible but that should not be a problem for anyone – except for you, of course.'

I was twisting the tiger's tail. The dynamics of our relationship had changed dramatically. He knew it, and I knew it. I stood up and faced him. 'Look, Schmitt,' I heard myself saying, 'I don't want to waste my time talking politics with you. I agree with you on some things – and I don't like cops. But, truth to tell, I don't particularly like you either – after what you did to Eoin, and what you would like to do to me too. What I told you about lodging these photographs with a solicitor in Dublin is true, plus the bit about me having to collect them in person, and also the bit about, if anything happens to me, the photos go straight to the French police. What do you think I did all that for?'

Before he could answer, I continued. 'Well, first of all, let's talk about you. I don't know why you sent me those photos. I said to you earlier that I was touched by your gesture. Yeah, well that was a lie. I never thought like that, and, having had the pleasure of meeting you in the flesh, I am now sure that you are a thoroughly evil and dangerous criminal, without even the excuse of being a lunatic. Medical researcher – huh? Well that's a laugh, anyhow! You are just the sickest, saddest sadist that I have ever met!'

He made a move to hit me again, but I was standing up this time and I parried the blow easily. I knew I was playing with fire, but there was method in my madness. He was believing me, precisely because I was telling him that I had been lying to him earlier in the afternoon – which, of course, I had – and still was.

The hard fact was that I needed to convince this ruthless killer that the photograph he needed was really in Dublin, out of his reach, and that the only way he could get his hands on it was to allow me to walk out of that house a free man. Under divine or diabolical inspiration, I had found the chink in this blood-sucker's armour. It was very simple. The way to convince him that I was actually telling the truth about everything else, was to speak to him with brutal candour about himself. I would guess that it was a very long time since anybody else had dared to do that. Was I courageous? No, just lucid. I clearly saw that this was the only way to save my own skin. I went for it, full throttle.

'I have thought a lot about why I got those photos in the post. Did you send them to me to gloat, to turn the knife in the wound about Eoin? Eventually, I decided that a killer would not bother to do that. So I got to thinking that it wasn't you who sent me the photos, but somebody who hoped I would go to the police, so that you would be punished for what you did to Eoin.

Are you hearing me, huh?'

He said nothing, but he had turned an interesting colour.

'When you searched my room from top to bottom, I guessed what you were after. Fortunately, I had brought the photographs with me to Mont Sainte-Odile – precisely in order to brood about what I should do with them. When I got back and saw that you had ransacked my room, I sent those photos to my solicitor with the instructions I have told you about. I did this for my own protection, because I had seen what you did to Eoin, and I was bloody well determined that you were not going to do the same thing to me.'

Schmitt hissed through icy, angry teeth: 'It was not me who searched your room.'

'Don't lie to me!' I retorted – the kettle calling the pot black – and how! 'You must be the only guy I know who wears Jeyes Fluid as an after-shave lotion. My place was reeking with the stuff when I got back from the Vosges – and so does this place, here and now. You really should consult a beautician – and about your insides even more than your outside.'

I was being witty, because he so obviously disliked people with a sense of humour, and did not know how to handle them. I sensed that this incomprehension increased my chances of deceiving him.

'What do you want?' he snarled.

I replied immediately, 'Money, a lot of money.' Money is usually a powerful sign that somebody is not joking. That is what I wanted him to think.

'Are you blackmailing me – for money?' he asked, in quiet fury.

'Are you blackmailing me – for my life?' I responded, almost cheerfully.

We looked at each other with detestation, and, I would like

to think, a degree of mutual, if grudging, respect. I said, 'We have in the Irish language a proverb that goes "*Aitnig cíaróg cíaróg éile*". It means "One cockroach recognises another". I think we can do business, without taking things to heart. I could have gone to the police when I received those photos. But what good would that have done for Eoin? No good at all. He is dead. I don't accept all your ballyhoo about being at war, and the heroic struggle. You are just a common cut-throat on the run. Well, I'm prepared to "facilitate" you – to put it respectably. Bottom line, it will cost you twenty thousand pounds. That is about a quarter of a million francs – nouveaux francs, of course. It is a bit more than that, actually, but what the hell! I'll settle for a quarter of a million.

We haggled about money. I did not yield an inch.

'Good Lord, a quarter of a million is chicken feed for the Third Reich. It is the least that they could do for you after all the poor devils that you have mutilated and murdered for them.'

He gave me two answers, neither of which I will ever forget. His first answer was to say soberly and, I think, sincerely, 'Your friend Eoin was a very different person from what you are. I told him much worse things than I have told you. Yet, for the short time he was in my car, he gave me a sense of peace, and even hope. I actually stopped the car and put him out because I wanted to spare him. I was even prepared to take that risk. If only he had not taken that photograph. I had no alternative then. I turned the car, drew level with him again, and told him that it had been good to talk to him, and that I needed to talk some more, and would he, please, sit into the car again. He was uneasy. He probably guessed that I had seen him taking the photograph. He said that he wanted to relieve himself and went a few yards down a side road. He was most likely wondering what to do, playing for time. I slipped out of the car and killed him while he was pissing. It was instantaneous and painless. It hurt me to have to kill him.'

I mimed playing a violin, and retorted – in English – with an obscenity so vile that I wouldn't even know how to say it in French.

That was the only thing I did or said that night that I regretted afterwards. In fairness, I think that Schmitt was sincere when he said that it hurt him to kill Eoin. Whatever tenuous hope he may have for salvation – in about a million years' time, of course – might very well hang on that ineffectual hurt feeling.

The second answer that Schmitt gave me, and which I will never forget either, was that he called the two goons into the room again and gave them some instructions in a low voice. Then, he sat and watched while they set about giving me the beating of my life.

Huge punches rained down upon me. Schmitt had obviously told his stooges not to punch my face or break any bones. After all, such injuries would look suspicious if I was going to visit my solicitor in the near future. That cheerful thought made the beating easier to bear.

One pinned my arms behind my back, and held my head up by a fistful of hair.

The other delivered great open-handed slaps to my face, so violent as to jerk my head a hundred and eighty degrees from side to side. I must have looked like someone watching a tennis rally at the French Open. Then both torturers lashed me with their fists, knees, even their boots, on the muscles of my upper arms, calves, and thighs, and into my stomach, crotch, and even anus, which I would have thought so anatomically inaccessible as to enjoy immunity. These animals were experts, and so sick as to know how to hurt, humiliate, and dehumanise, and refrain from killing, maiming, or leaving any mark on body surfaces visible to the public.

I don't know how long the beating lasted. I do know that when it was at its full fury, I was so winded that I could not even scream or cry out. When it was over, they dragged me upstairs – hauling me by the armpits, my feet stumbling on every step – and flung me onto the bed. I lay there, hurting, dazed, and deeply shocked. After a time, I started to sob. It was not so much the pain of the beating. It was the realisation that other human beings could actually do these things to me – or to anyone – expertly and systematically. I found this extraordinarily shocking and upsetting. We know that brutality and savagery exist, but only somebody who has been deliberately tortured by other breathing and sentient human beings knows the full horror of it.

And why had Schmitt set his mad dogs loose on me? At least I knew the answer to that one. It was because he was stinking drunk, because of pure rage at the things that I had said to him, and also out of frustration at the fact that he could neither torture me properly nor kill me, at least until I had visited my solicitor, and recovered the vital photograph. Above all, it was cold fury at the realisation that I had out-witted him and won, and that I was actually going to walk out of that house alive, and, in some sense, free.

I fell asleep, almost happy – if not particularly proud – that I was a really superlative liar.

CHAPTER SIXTEEN

I slept right through the night and woke up at seven o'clock the next morning, still fully dressed, on top of the bed where I had been dumped. I was sore from the beating I had got, but I was strangely peaceful – and even grateful. Grateful! A strange word in the context. Grateful for what? Grateful, I suppose, for the fact that I had survived, and had not disgraced myself by snivelling, begging my tormentors to stop, or even asking them or Schmitt why they were doing this to me. That was not because I was tough or courageous. It was more to do with having a basic sense of my own worth, of my own dignity – if the word is not too pompous. It was like when we were beaten in school, before corporal punishment was abolished in Ireland – you would die before you would cry.

I was grateful, above all, not to have mentioned Marianne. I had come within a hair's breadth of doing so when I was working overtime to concoct fairy tales about where the photographs currently were. I had nearly said, 'Oh, I left them in my girlfriend's apartment.' I realised now that if I had as much as suggested that to Schmitt, he would have had her kidnapped too, brought her here, and tortured her before my eyes, until I coughed up everything about the photographs. Then, once he knew that I had given the photos to the police, but that the registration number of his car had been burnt off by the flames, he would have killed us both and dumped the bodies in the Rhine.

I got up and was taking a shower when Fat Ass brought my breakfast. I wrapped a towel around myself hastily and went out to see who it was. I had already inspected my body in the bathroom mirror. I was black and blue all over – except on my face and hands. The thug cannot have failed to see the results of his handiwork, bruises all over my torso, my shoulders, and my legs. He actually had the gall to wish me a 'Good morning.' I ignored him. Whether or not I agreed with his assessment of the weather, neither of us gave a shit. That is the one thing we had in common. I went back into the bathroom and finished my shower. I'd had no razor for most of the week. As I was a black-headed hairy creature in those days, I already had what would be called nowadays the beginnings of 'designer stubble'. It looked cool and very masculine – especially with the bruises on my body.

I ate with relish, which is strange to say because, while I shovelled in the food, I was wondering whether Schmitt intended to kill me after breakfast. I could interpret the beating I had got as a rejection of my generous offer to exchange one photograph for a quarter of a million francs. I even found myself speculating about whether the fact that the Romans flogged prisoners before they crucified them was, in fact, a primitive form of anaesthetic. I think the Chinese do the same thing to this day – or is it the Japanese? Beating their victims all the way to the place of execution?

Was it because I had been beaten, that I found myself calm,

and curiously unafraid about the prospect of my own death? I thought about my parents, about Marianne, and about Eoin, with great love – but without getting emotional or allowing it to spoil my breakfast. If this was to be my 'last supper', I thought, let me at least enjoy it.

Schmitt came in at about ten o'clock.

'Did you sleep well?' he inquired. I did not answer. He went on, 'Listen, young fellow, you have had a bad experience. It was necessary, to put down a marker. You will have no long-term injuries. My – he hesitated about what to call his thugs – 'My *associates* are highly skilled and careful. So get over it.'

That annoyed me.

'Will you fuck off!' I replied in pure Dublinese. Perhaps he did not understand the language – or the subtlety of my thought – because he continued unperturbed.

'I will not give you a quarter of a million francs for your photograph. I will give you half that amount. I will also pay for your return journey to Dublin. I expect you to complete the round trip, Strasbourg-to-Strasbourg, in the space of one day, via Paris, no doubt. I will book the tickets for you myself. You will be – not exactly accompanied but, shall we say – supervised by an expert in the field of such operations. You will travel to and from Dublin airport and your solicitor's office by taxi with your supervisor, and you will not, in any way, make contact with your family or with any other person. This is not a family or a social visit: strictly business.'

My heart leapt as I listened to the ridiculous terms and conditions that the idiot was trying to impose on me. The only relevant part of what he was saying, from my point of view, was that I was actually going to walk out of that house alive and travel to Dublin. I could foresee that, when final arrangements were being made, I would be told that the 'supervisor' would choose a suitably secluded place in which to receive the photograph, and to pay over the money. He would not, in fact, receive the photograph – which, of course, was not in Dublin at all – and even if he did receive a photograph, he would not pay over any money. Instead he would lodge a bullet in my brain, and then return to France that same evening, no doubt tired but happy.

I vowed not to let that scenario happen either. Of one thing I was certain: as a Dub – born, bred, and brought up in that city – I could run rings around any supervisory stooge the Nazi cared to nominate.

'Money up front,' I challenged.

He smiled condescendingly and replied, 'I am sure that we can make a civilised arrangement which will be satisfactory to both of us. I will keep my word to you, as a soldier and a man of honour.'

I nearly puked to hear him say that. But he had something else to say.

'I have just spoken of putting down markers. That is what we were doing last night when we thought it prudent to demonstrate faintly but nonetheless graphically how deep would be our disappointment – indeed our disapproval – if you were so foolish as to seek to double-cross us.'

I sensed that when he said 'we', 'our', and 'us', he was not really including the goons downstairs. He was merely seeking to dilute, in some way, the disgust that he knew he inspired in me now. He continued in much plainer language.

'I need to be very clear about what will happen to you if you go to the police now or at any time in the future. We have a very long arm, and we are also very unforgiving. Sooner or later, my people will catch up with you – wherever you may be in the world. When they do get you, I promise, it will take you fully thirty action-packed days to die. You have ten fingers on your hands and ten toes on your feet, two eyes, and two ears, a nose and a tongue, two lips on your head, two test – '

I shouted him down,

'You are raving mad – and disgusting!'

He persisted, 'Thirty days. You will pray for those thirty days to be over, so that you can at last die. So if it helps you to avoid making a tragic mistake, be my guest, go straight ahead and believe that I am, as you say, "Raving mad – and disgusting."'

Paradoxically, my absolute loathing for this creature was such that it came almost naturally to me to conceal it from him. With cold deliberation and, indeed, smiling with all my teeth, I sought to reassure him – the better to double-cross him in the end.

'Look, if I have not been to the police by now, why would I go to them in the future? Eoin is dead. We cannot bring him back. I'll just take my money and go. A quarter of a million, incidentally, and no half-measures – I insist.'

He did not argue any more about money. Why should he? Since he did not plan to give me any money at all. Instead he asked me for details of my solicitors in Dublin. I gave him the name and address of the biggest firm of solicitors that I knew.

By a convenient coincidence, my father had just concluded prolonged and excruciating negotiations with this firm relating to the administration of the estate of the dotty grand aunt of mine who had bankrolled my studies. That law firm's premises, which I had visited a few times with my long-suffering Dad, were just made for losing any supervisor that Schmitt could appoint. The so-called supervisor would probably be found dead two years later in the basement, suffocated beneath as much red tape as there is seaweed in the Sargasso Sea.

I had to skate over some thin ice when it came to giving a name of the partner or the assistant who had charge of my photographs. I answered brazenly, 'Mr Foley', knowing full well that Mr Foley had died six months earlier, which sad event my father had greeted at the time as a particular sign of God's favour.

Schmitt drove off that afternoon, presumably back to Strasbourg to arrange for my journey to Dublin, and to recruit a suitable minder. Watching him through the window, I noted that he had removed his swastika armband.

'Back to the real world!' I exclaimed out loud into empty air. How I wished I could go with him. Instead, I settled down to seemingly interminable hours and – as it turned out – days, of worrying, hoping, and fearing.

The key question seemed to be at what precise point I should raise the red flag of rebellion. I could wait until I got to Dublin. Schmitt's minder would cling to me like a leech the whole way to the door of my solicitor's private consulting room, but he could not cross the threshold of that room with me. I could explain everything to the solicitor in a few deft phrases, and let him set the wheels in motion for the arrest of my minder outside in the waiting room, with the inevitable domino effect of rounding up Schmitt, his two goons, Blum, and God knows who else – the rest of the Nazi Party in France, in Europe, in the entire world. Why not?

On the other hand, that sounded like a top-heavy agenda for a solicitor's office on a business-as-usual day, particularly in the context of wild talk about an imaginary packet of photographs that nobody had ever heard of. The solicitor might be more inclined to hand me back to my minder – who could be counted on to make all the appropriate noises. The minder would receive stern instructions from my solicitor not to let me loose again, ever; those instructions would be followed to the letter.

So, I might be better to try and lose myself in the stairways and corridors of the solicitor's office, or even to get out the window of the room where my consultation would be held. Due apologies would be given for the discourtesy of leaving so peremptorily, provided, of course, that the current room was not on the tenth floor.

I could not keep myself from crazy and compulsive planning. The strain of the last few days had been considerable. I had known at every moment that my life was in imminent danger. If necessity is the mother of invention, I had invented obsessively, and had, in fact, played a blinder, convincing Schmitt that my inventions were realities. I had clawed, inch by inch, back from the jaws of death. Now, so near and yet so far, I realised that if I made one false move, one miscalculation, the results could still be nasty, brutal, and very short. So, my mind was still in overdrive, probing all the variables, all the possibilities.

For instance, why should I wait to get to Dublin? There were no regular direct flights from Strasbourg to Dublin in those days. The local airport was Entzheim. From there one flew to Le Bourget, and then on to Dublin. At some point – perhaps even before I left Entzheim – the Waffen SS were going to have to loosen their grip on me. Why then couldn't I hand myself over to the police there, asking to be taken into protective custody for as long as it took me to explain myself. If they refused, I could always commit a helpful crime – like breaking a window or blatantly stealing something from one of the airport shops.

Schmitt thought that I would meekly travel to Dublin, because I was greedy for his money. It would be fun to disappoint him. And anyhow, as I have said, I was certain that he had no intention of giving me anything except a bullet in the head once he had collected his photograph. Just as I, too, had no intention of giving him anything – certainly not a photograph, which, in any case, I didn't even have. So, two liars, determined to double-cross one another. Honour among thieves – as we used to say in auld Dublin.

I had another reason not to want to travel to Dublin. Although I had been able eventually to take showers, I had been dressed in the same clothes, shirt, underwear, and socks – day and night – for most of the last week. They were filthy – firstly from lying in the van, then from prolonged wear, and also from the savage beating I had received the night before. This had caused me to, shall I say, vent some strong emotions in my pants. I could not help it. And I had not shaved in days. I am not particularly vain but, if only for the sake of other passengers, I could not dream of travelling anywhere looking – and smelling – like that.

Schmitt did not return the same day. When he had not returned by the following evening, I began to have another set of compulsive worries. Perhaps the police investigation into the murder of his wife had made progress, and the link to Eoin's killing had become clearer. Perhaps they had arrested Schmitt already. This would be good news for the cause of justice, but very bad news for me. If Schmitt did not come back to Struthof from Strasbourg – because he had been arrested, or for any other reason – what instructions, if any, had he left to his pair of chimpanzees about what to do with me? Or, in default of instructions, what would they do, left to their own initiative? That might be the most volatile and dangerous situation of all.

I had a sort of deal with Schmitt. I had little doubt that he intended to double-cross me, once I had handed over the photographs, but I planned on double-crossing him even before we got that far. On the other hand, I had no *entente cordiale* with Schmitt's herd of oxen. Having had a free sample of what they were capable of when they were brutalising me, I did not expect them to show any mercy if it was left to them to decide what to do.

I suppose that it did not help either that diplomatic relationships were broken off since the night that they had beaten me up. I would not demean myself to ask either of them questions or to ask them for anything at all. When they brought me food, I turned my back on them. I ate the food, of course, but I did not say either please or thank you; I certainly did not say 'Have a nice day!'

My sober guess was that if the gruesome twosome got wind that Schmitt was in trouble, they would immediately destroy as much evidence as they possibly could – starting with me. Ruthlessness was the hallmark of their organisation and the secret of their surprising virulence decades after the war. They would certainly kill me out of hand, and especially as it would more than likely emerge that I had lied through my teeth to their boss, and was even now planning to double-cross him – and so them – yet again.

If it was to happen, I reasoned, it would happen by night. Asleep, I would be at my most defenceless. It is also much easier to dispose of a body by dark of night, when tourists or hikers are much less likely to be wandering around in the forest.

On the second night, they cut off the heating. I took this as a sinister omen that departure was imminent: for them, to whatever rat-run they normally inhabited, and for me, to some place over the rainbow. In the jittery state I was in, it never even occurred to me that the boiler might simply have broken down, or run out of oil. I slept in an armchair that night. The cold was enough to keep me from falling into a deep sleep. I had made up my mind that if I heard menacing sounds outside my door in the middle of the night, I would quickly position myself close to it, and break the skull of any prospective assassin who was rash enough to come in. For that purpose, I had armed myself with a golf club which I had found at the back of a wardrobe. What to do if there were two prospective assassins, I frankly did not know. I suppose I hoped naively that the second guy would be polite, and simply wait for his turn to get his skull split.

CHAPTER

SEVENTEEN

Schmitt came back on the third day – a Wednesday, as I recall – in the late afternoon. He seemed in no hurry to see me, but I could hear him talking with his sidekicks. I could not make out any words but I had two main impressions. Anger – something had gone wrong – and determination – something needed to be put right, and Schmitt was just the man to do it. I tried to fit myself into either scenario, and came up with nothing. Since I had been captured, I had only been able to react to what had been happening to and around me. In so far as I had made plans at all, I had not had an opportunity to share those plans with anyone else. Nobody could have either betrayed my intentions, or even been annoyed by what I proposed to do. In the time that had elapsed, the police may have accused Schmitt of murdering his own wife. But that was nothing to do with me. It only meant that Schmitt would be more anxious than ever to regain possession of Eoin's photographs. Fortunately, the police had not taken him into custody, so my trip to Dublin – or at least to Entzheim – would still be on. That would be my only chance to escape alive from this house. I would indeed be one of the few lucky people to survive a stay at Struthof.

Towards evening on the same day, the two oafs suddenly erupted into my room. For a moment, I thought that they were going to beat me again. Instead, they stood me up and tied my arms behind my back. My mind raced ahead. Why were they doing this? Surely the authorities at Entzheim would not accept a passenger trussed up like a Christmas turkey? Perhaps, I guessed wildly, they would have forged papers proving that I was a criminal being repatriated to Ireland, to stand trial for armed robbery or piracy on the high seas. It occurred to me that they would need my passport, which was still in Strasbourg – unless, of course, the obliging Madame Blum had provided them with it. I was sure that she knew, even better than myself, where everything was in my room.

My warders nudged me gently towards the door. It was their gentleness that alerted me. Something was very wrong. Suddenly, my heart was in my mouth. No need to ask them; I could guess the rest. They got me downstairs. Schmitt was waiting. He did not look at me. Another bad sign. Every criminal lawyer knows that the members of a jury who have just decided to condemn a murderer to death never look at the accused as they file back into court.

'You lied to me,' Schmitt said curtly. I did not make any reply. He continued. 'Did you really think that we don't have sympathisers in the police force; people who will tell us things?'

He waited for an answer. He did not get one.

'I know now that you delivered those photographs to the police station at Avenue de la Foret Noire in Strasbourg, to be conveyed to a certain Inspector Péron at Orléans. I know also that the photographs were so damaged by fire that it was impossible to identify my car from them.'

'Well, what are you worried about, so?' I said lamely.

'I am not worried about anything,' he retorted. 'It is you who should be worried – very worried. I despise liars, especially liars who are only interested in money. At least your little friend Eoin did not sink as low as that.'

Everything about this sneering reply annoyed me – the accusation that I was only interested in money, the insinuation that I was a despicable liar, when he, as the murderer of my best friend, and someone who was actively planning to murder me as well – had no possible right to hear the truth. Most especially, I resented his contemptuous reference to Eoin as my 'little friend'. I knew perfectly well what he meant by that. It vexed me, as much for Eoin's sake as for my own. Who the hell was Schmitt to despise or sneer at anybody, for any reason? I kept my speech from the dock short and to the point.

'*Va te faire foutre!*', which means exactly what you think it means.

It was actually helpful to me that Schmitt had insulted me, and provoked me to respond in the same coinage. It meant that I had to die bravely, and not waste my breath on begging for mercy or trying to cut some abject deal. If these had to be my last words – though perhaps I should have preferred something more soulful or profound – I was not ashamed of them. They would do very well. Eoin would never have said such a thing himself. Still, I knew that he was smiling there or, well, somewhere in the time/space continuum. I asked him to help me to die decently, and – as I did not want to die blubbering – I also asked him to use his influence to make sure that I would not even think of my parents, or my sister, or Marianne until five minutes after I was dead.

Schmitt signalled to the oxen. One of them opened the door. Immediately outside, propped against the wall of the house, were a spade and a shovel. I practically threw up when I saw that. 'You miserable pack of bastards!' I thought. 'Couldn't you have had the common decency not to let me see those things?' On his way past, Fat Ass lovingly scooped up the instruments of my interment. Clearly, they had no plans to wake me in traditional Irish style. On the contrary, I was to be buried warm, like a cat buries its shit. I might even be disabled, stunned, but not actually dead. No matter. Out of sight is out of mind. There was little likelihood that, with my arms tied behind my back and a bullet lodged in my brain, I could fight my way up through three or four feet of stones and soil.

We walked a few hundred yards from the house. 'Of course' – I found myself reflecting automatically – 'they did not want to shoot me – or whatever they planned to do – in the house. That would make a terrible mess.' I knew, too, that they would make a major effort to conceal the fact that I had ever been in that house at all. I had seen how important it had been for Eoin's parents that we had found his body. It made me very lonely to realise that my own body would probably never be found, and that my parents and Marianne would never know for sure what had become of me, or even whether or not I was dead. I tried not to think about this.

We had arrived in a small clearing among the trees. Schmitt asked me if I wanted a blindfold. I thought it was a ridiculous question, so I did not answer. He drew a handgun out of his pocket and put it to my head – to my temple. I don't know much about guns. This one was quite small, but adequate – as I was to learn – to blow my brains out. I shut my eyes. You do that instinctively when you are expecting a loud noise close to your ear. There was a bright flash. I thought, in rapid succession, that I had been shot, then, that it had been painless, and, finally, that the whole performance had been a dismal anti-climax.

I opened my eyes again – to a scene like one of these '*son et lumière*' things at a chateau in the Loire Valley – brighter than day. I had to blink rapidly several times. We had the *lumière* bit; the *son* was soon to follow. When it came, it was like the public-address system at a by-election in rural Ireland, 'full of sound and fury, and signifying nothing'. There was a series of high-pitched screeches, followed by an encore of crackling sounds, as if there was a forest fire blazing in the neighbourhood. Finally, there was coherent speech.

'Attention! Attention! This is a police announcement. Repeat, this is a police announcement. Put down your guns. I say put down your guns. The police are armed and you are surrounded. You have been warned. The police are armed and you are surrounded. Put down that gun. Josef Schmitt, Georges Dupuy, you are under arrest. Put down that gun.'

My mind was in total gridlock – traffic-jam mode. I had so many conflicting thoughts and emotions in that moment that I attended to none of them individually. Instead, I found myself doing a literary critique of the police announcement. I decided that it was drab, boring, and repetitive. I thought, too, that it was a bit pompous to call it a 'Police Announcement' when it was really only addressed to one or two people. I did not have a gun to put down, so it was not addressed to me. I knew, to my cost, who Josef Schmitt was. But which of the other two stooges was Georges Dupuy? And was the other one not to be arrested too? I found that this was not quite fair. They had both kidnapped me, held me prisoner, and beaten me up. What is sauce for the goose is sauce for the gander, *n'est-ce pas*?

It took me a few seconds to realise that I had more urgent preoccupations than such trivial pursuits. Schmitt's revolver was cold on my temple. At the first flare of light, he had jerked it convulsively from the side of my head into my forehead. It occurred to me, spontaneously, that he was going to blow away the frontal lobe of my brain – instead of a lateral one. I did not suppose that it could make much difference. I would end up just as dead as you can get. In the meantime, the awkward fool seemed to have scraped inches of skin off my forehead with the snout of his pistol. 'Clumsy whore!' I exclaimed out loud. It was sore.

Suddenly, he fired at point-blank range. I felt nothing – except shock, and deafness. That is strange, I thought, I have always heard that when people are dying, the faculty of hearing is the last to go. There was blood everywhere. I could drown in the stuff, I thought, though that would hardly be necessary, I remembered a nano-second later. I was surely dead already. Then I felt Schmitt behind me, pushing me, even flinging me roughly to the ground. I thought indignantly that this was typical of the boor, and just another example of his ignorant attitude to people. I was dead, or as good as dead anyhow – I knew that – but could he not even wait for me to lie down in my own time?

★

Schmitt had shot himself in the mouth. This accounted for how I was suddenly drenched in blood, and also for the rude shoving sensation I had felt 'in my last moments'. The man, literally, fell dead on top of me. The bullet must have passed within inches of my face. I did not realise it at the time, but the police told me afterwards that, as Schmitt was holding the gun to my head in his right hand, his left arm had been around my neck. Our two faces were practically touching. Fortunately for me, he chose the right mouth when it came to saying, 'Open wide!' Schmitt did not have any mouth a fraction of a second later, as he blew half his own head off.

'We did not dare to shoot, for fear of getting you,' Inspector Péron told me later. 'Otherwise, we would certainly have taken him out. It's policy, you know, zero tolerance for anybody threatening somebody else with a firearm.'

'That's nice to know,' I said sardonically.

The two oafs made a ridiculous attempt to run away. Not built for either speed or heights, they both had to be rescued from the same outcrop of rock on the mountainside, where, like cats in a tree, they had got themselves out on a limb. I enjoyed the spectacle. Fat Ass gave a particularly enchanting performance, as if incarnating the very nickname that I had spontaneously chosen for him. He really did shake his ass whole-heartedly. Even the dourest of people have a latent talent for slapstick comedy. They were hating every moment of it, of course. That made it even funnier.

★

Inspector Péron drove me back to Strasbourg. He was a man of leisure until the next day, as the Strasbourg police were in charge of mopping-up operations. I was due to turn up the next afternoon at the Préfecture to make a statement, and for a detailed debriefing about all that I had learnt during my captivity. Inspector Péron would, of course, attend that session, though he probably would not have any more investigating to do into the two murders with which he had been concerned – that of Eoin and of Schmitt's wife – because the perpetrator was, presumably, facing an even more searching inquiry where he had chosen to go.

On the way, the Inspector answered some of my questions.

'Yes, Mademoieselle Marianne reported to the Strasbourg police that you were missing. They knew, of course, of my interest in Eoin Macklin's case. You may be sure that Mlle Marianne forcefully reminded them of it.'

'That's my gal!' I murmured happily.

'I dropped everything, and came straight away.'

I thanked him, and he said that it was '*normal*', which is the French for 'Don't mention it'.

'When we were last in contact,' the Inspector continued, 'I told you that we had a suspect – the owner of a big black Renault, whose wife had died in suspicious circumstances. We began to investigate this guy. The car was registered in the name of Josef Schmitt. That is a very common name in Alsace, but not in Aveyron, where he is living now. In fact, the wife is – or was – a local woman, but Schmitt himself is – or was – a blow-in. Nobody seemed to know much about him. That interested me.

'Playing a hunch, I checked, by telegram, with the Simon

Wiesenthal Centre in Vienna, to see whether there was a Josef Schmitt on their books. We quite often do that nowadays, when things don't add up – for people in a certain age-bracket. Well, the Wiesenthal people came up with a resistance fighter called Josef Schmitt, who disappeared in 1942. He was thought to have been liquidated in Struthof. There were many such people, both men and women, who simply disappeared in Struthof during the war. You do realise – don't you – that Struthof is where you were held prisoner and where we are just coming from now?'

'Yes, of course,' I replied.

'Well, Strasbourg, Struthof, a dead member of the Maquis called Josef Schmitt, and a live person suspected of wife-murder, also called Josef Schmitt, who owned a big black Renault: that all began to make some kind of sense.'

I broke in excitedly: 'You can say that again! Schmitt told me himself that he stole the name Josef Schmitt from a *maquis-ard*, who had been hanged in Struthof during the war. He also told me all I know about the Wiesenthal Centre in Vienna. He was not at all complimentary about those people.'

Péron laughed. 'You can bet your sweet life he wasn't! Did he tell you his own real name, his pre-war name?'

'No, he refused to tell me that. But he did tell me what he had been doing at Struthof during the war: medical experiments – of the most disgusting kind. Incredibly, he seemed to think that he was a cross between Louis Pasteur and Madame Curie.'

'*Mon Dieu*,' the Inspector exclaimed admiringly, 'you have found out a lot – single-handedly – haven't you! So, let me tell you something else. The Simon Wiesenthal Centre telephoned me the following day, saying that they were interested in our Josef Schmitt. They told me – something that is already fairly well known in police circles – that, as the war was drawing to a close, several Nazis were running for cover, for fear of well-deserved reprisals. Those who were in a position to do so sometimes assumed the identities of people who had disappeared during the war. As Schmitt, a member of the Maquis, was believed to have been executed in Struthof, the Wiesenthal people had conducted a search of their records to see what prominent Nazis were missing from Struthof at the end of the war. They came up with a guy called Georges Dupuy. Of course, if Schmitt is a common name in Alsace, Dupuy, or Dupuis with an 's', is an even more common name throughout the length and breadth of France.

So what was Georges Dupuy up to during the war at Struthof? Exactly as you have described it: gruesome medical experiments. The Weisenthal people say that he did not have any medical qualifications at all. They have statements from survivors saying that he did the most atrocious things. But he simply vanished at the end of the war. A lot of those guys have sunk without trace. They seem to have their own very effective network. We think that most of them are in South America by now, living under false identities.'

'That's your guy, all right,' I exclaimed. 'He didn't give me his name, but he confessed to me what he had been doing – or rather – he *boasted* openly. Of course, that was when he had already decided to kill me.'

After a few moments of sucking his teeth reflectively and changing gear, the Inspector asked me whether I thought that Schmitt or Dupuy, or whatever his name was, had told Eoin Macklin the same things when he had had him in his car.

'Yes, I am sure that he did. In fact Schmitt told me himself that he had told Eoin much worse things. He actually used that expression. So, that means he knew bloody well that what he was doing was disgusting.'

'One thing that does seem certain is that they are the same person. I shouted both names over the loudhailer. It was when I shouted "Georges Dupuy" – that is precisely the moment when he shot himself. He knew then that the game was up. Have you heard of Adolf Eichmann?'

'Of course. Schmitt said that he was a great genius of social engineering,' I answered.

'He would say that, wouldn't he?' the Inspector commented drily. 'Well, since Eichmann, these guys cannot stand the thought that they could be handed over to the Israelis, and be hanged by them. The mere thought of it drives them frantic.'

We were approaching Wolfisheim, the outskirts of Strasbourg. I said to the Inspector, 'I have plenty more questions to ask you. Why don't you come up to Marianne's apartment? We can all go out to dinner together.'

'Oh, I wouldn't dream of intruding,' Péron replied.

'No,' I insisted, 'I am sure you are at a loose end this evening. Besides, I'll need a chaperon. Marianne will be so glad to see me, she will be certain to molest me, if you don't come up.'

The Inspector looked startled. He shook his head, puzzled.

'You Irish have a very strange sense of humour. We never know when you are joking and when you are serious.'

'Well, I wish I was serious about the chances of being molested, but I am very serious about asking you up.'

He weakened. I asked him to drive by my flat first, so that I could get a quick shower and a change of clothes. On the way in, we encountered Madame Blum, who wore her usual rigor mortis expression and did not seem pleased to see me – back from the dead.

'Did you miss me?' I inquired brightly and provocatively.

I think she actually farted with surprise – at the greeting as much as the apparition. She certainly made a noise – somehow. I sniffed, and went on trying to jolly her up.

'This is Police Inspector Péron. You may be seeing more of him.'

She simpered and giggled nervously – very unlovely, both the sight and the sound of it. We went up hastily.

Fifteen minutes later, we were at Marianne's apartment. I won't try to describe the welcome we got.

'Didn't I tell you that I needed police protection?' I said to the Inspector, when we were seated, with celebratory kirs *au vin d'Alsace*.

I asked him how the police had found me – just in the nick of time. I outlined the details for Marianne, and I did not have to exaggerate anything.

'Perhaps thirty seconds would have made the vital – or the mortal – difference. This bloody fellow already had a gun to my head, and he was certainly going to use it. I hope you are suitably horrified, sweetheart.'

Sweetheart was. She made those special gargling noises in her throat that French girls reserve for the horrific.

'It is complicated,' the Inspector began, 'or at least Alsace is complicated. By the time the war was over, quite a few people found themselves – shall we say – compromised. This applied especially to officials in the administration, or, for instance, in the police force. These were people who had been forced to do shameful things, or, at the very least, to turn a blind eye to what other people around them were doing. This was not just a question of Strasbourg, or Alsace. It was true, to a greater or lesser extent, of all of Vichy France as well. But the problems were far more acute in the annexed territories of Alsace and Lorraine.

If an individual case had been particularly serious or notorious, the authorities of the new French Republic could not give the people who had compromised themselves a soft landing after the war. There were reprisals, executions, prison sentences, and expulsions or forced retirements from the police force, as from other branches of the public service. There were other cases where, in fairness, it had to be admitted that people had done the best they could in the circumstances. There was an effort made to be realistic about such people – especially where they had come clean about what they had done.

Finally, there were grey-area people, guys who had gone seriously astray, to the extent that they could still be regarded as sympathisers by neo-Nazi groups. Some of these were recruited as double-agents, either as repentant sinners who had seen the light, or by the simplest means of all.'

'What is that?' I asked.

'Blackmail,' the Inspector replied comfortably, as if it were the most obvious thing in the world.

'Putting it crudely, these guys are given a choice: "Either face charges because of the dirt you did during the war, or become a spy for us." We tell them, "The tide has gone out for you, don't you think? We could give you a really bad time. But you still have active links to what have now become the subversives. Well, keep those links, and use them to keep us informed about what your shitty friends are up to." You owe your life, André, to such a double-agent.'

'I am flattered!' I exclaimed. 'How did it happen?'

The Inspector continued, carefully, not wanting to let too many cats out of the bag – perhaps just in case I might sell my story to the Sunday papers.

'Our double-agent is an elderly man, who did make mistakes during the war – which he regrets. He is still in the police force. Schmitt regarded him obviously as still a true believer in Nazism. So, he approached him with three very explicit questions. Had Monsieur André Olden handed the police a bunch of photographs? Secondly, how damaged were those photographs by fire? Thirdly, and very specifically, could the registration number of a car that appeared in one of those photos still be read?'

'*Nom d'un chien!*' I exclaimed. 'What reply did your famous double-agent make? At that stage I was just about hanging on to dear life by my fingernails, telling Schmitt that I had never given those photos to the police, and that I had sent them to my lawyer in Ireland, with strict instructions not to surrender them to anyone except myself, in person. That was the only way I could devise to get out of Struthof alive.'

'Ingenious – and very untruthful!' the Inspector chided – facetiously, I hope.

'So what did your brilliant double-agent tell Schmitt? My God! He spilled the beans, didn't he? I was dragging red herrings all over the place, proposing to sell the vital photo to Schmitt for a quarter of a million francs, if only he would let me go to Dublin to collect it. In fact, I had a big plan made to turn myself in to the police at Entzheim. I was fighting for my life – while you people were busy selling me down the Swanee!'

'Relax, *cher ami*.' Schmitt got our stock answer from the double-agent: 'Come back tomorrow; I'll try to find out for you in the meantime.' That gave us time to set up our own game-plan. When our guy reported back to us with the questions he had been asked, the matter was referred straight to myself, because the chiefs here knew of my interest in Eoin Macklin's case, and also in yours – I mean, your disappearance, as reported by Mademoiselle Marianne.

When Schmitt came back the following day, he was told that, yes, you had passed the photographs to the police. In fairness, Andrew, we did not realise that you had denied that. He was also told that, while nobody here knew the precise extent of the damage caused by the fire – because the investigation was being conducted by the police in Loir-et-Cher – that he must be in the clear, because if the registration number of the car was still visible, the police would have been on top of him within twenty-four hours.'

'*Merde alors!* Where did that leave me?' I protested.

'In so far as we knew, it left you in exactly the same position as you had been before that, namely that Schmitt was determined to get rid of you. That is what you said yourself, right?'

'Yes but . . . ' I protested.

'Yes, but, but, but,' the Inspector insisted, 'the twenty-four-hour delay meant that we were ready for him. Bright lights, loudhailers, a force of men armed to the teeth. All that was out of sight, of course. Also out of sight, but clinging like leeches, were four cars in radio contact to ring the changes on tailing Schmitt's car, when he had got his answer, and was heading back for Struthof. We never lost sight of him. It was made easier by the fact that our double-agent already knew about Schmitt's house in the Vosges. In fact, he had even been entertained there at least once. An ideal place, he said, to store people you wanted to kill when you got round to it.

We could have stormed the house. On balance, I decided that this would be more dangerous for you. Besides, we did not think that he would kill you in the house – too much fall-out from a killing, I mean, what with modern means of detection.'

'By "fall-out" you mean microscopic bits of me?' I inquired sarcastically.

'That is nicely put.' My sarcasm, apparently, had not penetrated the thermal underwear of his aplomb.

'If we could only get them out into the open, we could at least have had a sporting chance with a sharp-shooter to take out the bad lads. My instinct, as I say, was that they would not kill you in the house. I thought that they would drive away at nightfall, to an even more deserted place, where they would kill and bury you.'

'How nice!' I said, trying sarcasm half-heartedly a second time.

Marianne patted my wrist. She held me tight, and kissed me.

'Eoin was looking after you, remember,' she said softly.

My eyes were suddenly full of tears.

'Yes, I do remember, sweetheart. I will never, ever forget.'